THE BATTLE OF BAYPORT

HARDY BOYS ADVENTURES

#6 *THE BATTLE OF BAYPORT*

FRANKLIN W. DIXON

ALADDIN   New York London Toronto Sydney New Delhi

ALADDIN

An imprint of Simon & Schuster Children's Publishing Division
1230 Avenue of the Americas, New York, NY 10020
First Aladdin hardcover edition June 2014
Text copyright © 2014 by Simon & Schuster, Inc.
Jacket illustration copyright © 2014 by Kevin Keele
All rights reserved, including the right of reproduction in whole or in part in any form.
ALADDIN is a trademark of Simon & Schuster, Inc.,
and related logo is a registered trademark of Simon & Schuster, Inc.
THE HARDY BOYS MYSTERY STORIES, HARDY BOYS ADVENTURES,
and related logo are trademarks of Simon & Schuster, Inc.
Also available in an Aladdin paperback edition.
For information about special discounts for bulk purchases, please contact Simon & Schuster
Special Sales at 1-866-506-1949 or business@simonandschuster.com.
The Simon & Schuster Speakers Bureau can bring authors to your live event.
For more information or to book an event contact the Simon & Schuster Speakers Bureau
at 1-866-248-3049 or visit our website at www.simonspeakers.com.
Jacket design by Karin Paprocki
The text of this book was set in Adobe Caslon Pro.
Manufactured in the United States of America 0216 FFG
2 4 6 8 10 9 7 5 3
Library of Congress Control Number 2013948653
ISBN 978-1-4814-0007-7 (hc)
ISBN 978-1-4814-0006-0 (pbk)
ISBN 978-1-4814-0008-4 (eBook)

CONTENTS

THE BATTLE OF BAYPORT

FLASHBACK

1

FRANK

I T'S NOT EVERY DAY YOU GET TO SHOOT A CANNON at a regiment of eighteenth-century British redcoats. Not in the twenty-first century, at least. But for one day, my humble little town of Bayport had flashed back to the year 1776.

The park overlooking our town's namesake bay had been transformed into a battlefield with America and Great Britain facing off across center field of the baseball diamond to fight it out over freedom and taxes. Spectators decked out in Colonial garb watched from the bleachers and the hillside nearby, while a Benjamin Franklin look-alike grilled up hot dogs and hamburgers on the barbecue. In the port below, an American flag with only thirteen stars flew from the mast of a huge old Continental Navy warship. It was quite a sight.

I mean, seeing your family, friends, and classmates

1

carrying muskets and dressed up in 250-year-old military uniforms is about as strange as it gets. It felt kind of like the whole town had traveled back in time.

We were reenacting the Battle of Bayport to commemorate our town's small part in the Revolutionary War (it was more of a skirmish than a battle, really) and to celebrate the grand opening of the new Bayport History Museum aboard the USS *Resolve*, a beautifully restored sailing frigate from the very first US naval fleet.

The town had gone all out for the event, and it was hard not to get swept up in the excitement. Just about everyone in Bayport had turned out, and many of them were participating, my brother Joe and I included. The Revolutionary War had always been one of my favorite subjects. I was also volunteering at the museum along with the rest of Bayport High's Young Historians Club, so I have to admit that I felt a real sense of pride standing there in my militiaman uniform. Even Joe, who doesn't always share my more studious inclinations, had to admit that any event where you got to fire a real musket was pretty cool.

"Freedom schmeedom!" Joe yelled at me from across the field, apparently getting into character as a redcoat rifleman. "That's the last time I let you have the last doughnut, you ungrateful Colonial freeloader!"

Okay, so maybe Joe wasn't taking the reenactment as seriously as I was. But we weren't really here to fight over doughnuts. This was a celebration.

Last year the Bayport Historical Society found a whole stash of Revolutionary War armaments buried in the *Resolve*'s collapsed cargo hold when they started restoring the ship. There were crates and crates full of muskets, sabers, uniforms, and all kinds of other stuff. They even found the large Colonial flag now flying from the *Resolve*'s tallest mast, and military correspondence from General George Washington himself. It turns out the *Resolve* had been transporting supplies and marching orders to Continental troops in the South back in 1776 when the ship was attacked off the coast by the British fleet and run aground.

The *Resolve* had been a rotting wreck, but the stuff in the crates was in amazing condition. Everyone agreed the find was pretty much priceless. It was a huge deal in the history and archeology communities, and because of it our new history museum was going to be home to one of the world's most impressive collections of Revolutionary War artifacts. Historians, collectors, and enthusiasts were coming from all over the country for the museum's opening. One guy was even coming all the way from London.

My AP US History teacher, Mr. Lakin, who also happens to be the president of the historical society, had been the one to open the first crate. After the discovery, there had been a lot of debate about whether to preserve the items or just sell them all at auction for the money. Mr. Lakin finally convinced bigwig Bayport developer Don Sterling and the city council that turning the entire thing, the ship and all, into a world-class museum would do more for the town's economy than just selling everything off.

Judging by today's turnout, they had done the right thing. For the reenactment, Mr. Lakin had thankfully ditched his usual plaid-and-polyester outfit for a pristine Colonial general's uniform. He sat on top of a white horse looking over his troops, beaming with pride under his huge hat.

I was nearby, helping man one of the big cannons. We had a bunch of cannonballs piled in a neat pyramid next to the big old artillery gun, but we weren't going to be loading them. We were just going to go through the motions, only loading the cannon with a little gunpowder so we could still fire it and put on a good show without anyone actually getting blown to bits in the process. The infantrymen on the battlefield were basically just shooting blanks as well. Everyone agreed that firing live ammunition would have made the reenactment a little too historically accurate.

Well, almost everyone. I could think of a few participants who probably wouldn't mind shooting at each other. For a small town, we sure do manage to stir up our share of conflicts. Joe and I have witnessed plenty of them firsthand in our unofficial capacity as Bayport's foremost unlicensed private investigators. Getting mixed up in other people's beefs is a habit—either a good one or a bad one, depending on who you ask—and us Hardy boys can't seem to shake it, no matter how hard we try to mind our own business.

There were two people in particular who might like to

exchange shots, Mr. Lakin and Don Sterling. The local news even did a report on how their arguments over the best way to run the museum had nearly derailed the whole project. It seemed fitting that they were now facing off across the battlefield as opposing generals.

Joe and I found ourselves fighting on opposite sides of the battle as well. While I was behind the front line manning artillery for the good guys in blue, Joe was up front with the redcoat infantry's vanguard. Back in the day the two armies had their riflemen line up right out in the open in the middle of a field, like they were getting ready to play a football game or something. Only instead of kicking off a ball, they fired straight at each other with muskets and cannons until the side that was shot up the most either gave up or ran off. It was basically like two big firing squads having a shootout! And then sometimes, whoever was left standing would charge at each other with bayonets and fight hand to hand. Pretty crazy if you ask me.

Joe waved from across the baseball-diamond-turned-battlefield and gave me a salute. I'm pretty sure patriots and redcoats weren't supposed to salute one another before the battles, but I saluted him back anyway. He was my brother, after all.

Red, white, and blue fireworks burst in the air over the *Resolve*. It gave me the chills. It meant the battle was about to begin.

THE SHOT HEARD ROUND BAYPORT

2

JOE

KABOOM. **THE FIRST CANNON BLAST** thundered from the USS *Resolve*'s gun ports, announcing the official start of the reenactment of the Battle of Bayport. A big cheer went up from everyone. I could see Frank across the battlefield, waving the cannon's big ramrod in the air and whooping it up. My brother really gets into this stuff.

Frank signed up for the reenactment because he can be a bit of a nerd sometimes. Me, well, let's just say girls dig a guy in uniform. Yes, even one with a goofy tricorn hat that looks more like a giant pastry than headwear. At least, that's what I was hoping. There was one girl in particular I wanted to impress. Jen Griffin looked great all dolled up in her Colonial dress as she watched the reenactment with a group of our fellow costumed Bayport High classmates. I tipped my tricorn in her direction, and she smiled that beautiful smile. That girl really did a number on me. I think my cheeks might have turned as red as the wool coat I was wearing, and I hoped she didn't notice. To be honest, I was more interested in watching her watch the battle than actually participating in it.

The extra credit I was getting in Mr. Lakin's history class didn't hurt, though. I'm no slouch in the classroom, but I don't rack up the As quite as easily as Frank does. And Frank was right; it is pretty cool getting to fire a real musket. As underage, not to mention unlicensed, private detectives, it's not often you get a chance to carry a gun. Frank and I are usually armed with little more than our wits, so I was pretty excited to pack a piece for once, even if the piece in question was a four-foot-long 250-year-old musket without ammunition.

The reenactment had turned into something of a family affair for the Hardys. Our dad, retired Bayport crime-fighting legend Fenton Hardy, and aunt, active Bayport culinary legend Aunt Trudy, had gotten into the spirit as well. They were sitting on a hill above the "battlefield" along with a lot of other townspeople, dressed up in Colonial attire, watching the battle live. Dad looked ridiculous in his powdered wig, and Aunt Trudy, never one to let historical accuracy interfere with comfort, had accessorized her Betsy Ross costume with a deluxe beach chair topped by a red, white, and blue sun umbrella. The smartphone she was using to take a video of the reenactment was a modern touch as well.

It's kind of nuts that back in the old days people used to actually gather around to watch live battles like they were a spectator sport or a play in the park. I guess they had to do something to entertain themselves before baseball and movie theaters, but it's a pretty morbid pastime. Luckily, today's festivities were supposed to be a lot less gruesome.

Although, there were a lot of people who probably wouldn't mind whacking Don Sterling, whose history of cutthroat wheeling and dealing had earned him the nickname "the Don." The Don wasn't an actual mobster or anything like that, but he did have a reputation as one of Bayport's most ruthless, and stingiest, businessmen. The town was full of ex-business partners and employees he'd turned into enemies over the years.

The Don adjusted his long red coat and yelled, "Prepare for battle, gents!" in a bad British accent. Don Sterling was an enthusiastic member of the town's community theater, though everyone suspected his uncommonly generous donations had more to do with him landing leading roles than his acting chops.

Across the line, Mr. Lakin was trotting back and forth on his white horse, rallying the rebels. He actually looked a lot less ridiculous in his eighteenth-century general's uniform than he normally did in his, um, "contemporary" clothing. Old Man Lake, as some of the kids call him when he isn't around, hadn't updated his wardrobe since the early 1980s, and it was probably out of style even then. He was a devotee of the "Three Ps" school of fashion: lots of polyester, plaid, and pastels. And big collars. Lots of big collars. Lake was a hard teacher and it was just about impossible to get an A (unless you were Frank), but everyone still liked him because he was passionate about teaching and you knew he'd give you a fair deal if you worked hard.

Teachers rarely get the recognition they deserve, while guys with big bucks and political pull like the Don hog the limelight, so it was cool seeing Mr. Lakin front and center at such a big event. He was really soaking up all the attention too and enjoying the chance to steal some of the Don's thunder. I could hear him call out to his men from across the line.

"Don't fire until you see the whites of Sterling's beady little eyes!" he shouted out from atop his horse, earning whoops and hollers from his troops.

Don Sterling heard him too, and from the look on his face you could tell these guys really didn't like each other. The Don drew his saber.

"I'll cut you down myself, you rebel scum!" he screamed.

He had dropped the bad accent, and it sounded like he'd happily make good on his threat if he thought he could get away with it. Okay, so maybe the two men most responsible for our new history museum weren't making the most professional impression on Bayport's visitors, but us locals sure were enjoying the show.

"Attack!" the Don yelled, and the battle began in earnest. Across the line, I could hear our drama teacher, Mr. Carr, who was playing a Colonial sergeant, passionately ordering the militiamen to raise their muskets. The British officer next to me responded, shouting out the commands, "Make ready! Take aim!"

I shouldered my musket and took aim at a patch of grass a few feet in front of the football team's obnoxiously loud-mouthed lineman Mikey Griffin. Unfortunately, Mikey was Jen's big brother. And by big, I don't just mean older. The guy was huge. Fortunately, Jen got her looks from a different part of the Griffin gene pool.

"Fire!" shouted the officer. I pulled the trigger. The gun's flint-tipped hammer struck metal, igniting a flash of sparks in a little pan filled with gunpowder, and . . . *BOOM*. Flame and smoke leaped from the muzzle. The recoil wasn't a joke. It jolted my hands and slammed the wooden stock back into my shoulder. Man, what a rush. I wondered if Frank was feeling the same thing firing his cannon.

The officer yelled the order to reload, and we went through the surprisingly complicated ritual of reloading the old flintlock muskets. This bad boy wasn't like your modern guns, with self-contained bullets and multiple rounds. Even if you were only firing blanks, every time you wanted to shoot, you still had to go through the entire process of tearing open a paper cartridge full of gunpowder with your teeth and loading it straight down the barrel with a ramrod.

The whole thing took almost a minute—not including all those hours of gun safety training we had to complete before the museum's intimidating weapons specialist, Bernie Blank, would even let us pick up a musket. The paper cartridges in the leather ammunition pouches we'd been given to wear on our belts were missing the .75 caliber musket balls, of course, so no one would get shot for real. But even without any bullets, standing there all out in the open like that without any cover, hurrying to reload my musket while the enemy fired away and the cannons boomed, I realized how brave those guys must have been to stand there without running and face what had to seem like certain death.

This wasn't like the first-person-shooter video games Frank and I like to play, racking up points by blowing away zombies and aliens from our comfy gaming chairs. This was about as close as you could get to the real thing without it being the real thing. It was terrifying and exhilarating all at the same time. Looking out across the field through the haze of smoke with the smell of black powder and war cries filling the air, it stopped feeling like a reenactment. It was like I was really there, and for a second I knew what it must have felt like for those soldiers all those years ago, a lot of them still just kids my age, fighting for their country on the field of battle. Sure, I like to joke around a lot, but this was really profound stuff. Uh-oh, I better be careful. I'm starting to sound like my brother!

I wasn't the only one getting swept up in the action.

Mr. Lakin stormed through the ranks on his horse, waving a long flintlock pistol over his head, screaming, "Charge!"

All of us Bayport High kids cheered at that one, even those of us on the opposite side. It's not often you get to see your history teacher dressed up like George Washington, leading a charge on horseback.

Not wanting to be upstaged, Don Sterling ran forward, waving his saber over his head and yelling something about treachery and king's pride. I couldn't really hear him over all the noise. The patriots fired a final volley of shots, and Mr. Lakin let loose with his pistol. It jumped in his hand, and he almost fell off his horse. What a show!

Like we'd rehearsed, some of the soldiers on each side fell to the ground, pretending to be shot or wounded. The Don dropped to his knees with gusto, like he had really been shot. His hand groped for his heart, and he keeled over onto the ground. I hadn't remembered the British general getting shot during the rehearsal, or in the real battle for that matter, but overeager improvisation was one of the Don's calling cards as an amateur actor.

Following the Don's final flourish, the *Resolve*'s cannons boomed one more time, signaling the conclusion of the reenactment, and everyone cheered. Little did we know that the show was just getting started . . . the battle's real climax was still to come.

REWRITING HISTORY 3

FRANK

NOW, THAT WAS AWESOME. JOE AND I have had our share of adventures, but I've never gotten to experience anything quite like that before. It was like living history.

When the smoke cleared, everyone was milling around, talking excitedly and patting one another on the back. I saw Joe return his musket to Bernie Blank, who was collecting all the weapons to take back to the museum. Then he came over and put his arm around my shoulder.

"Man, I've got to give it to you, that was really amazing," he said.

"Huh?" I said, and Joe reached up and pulled out the earplugs I'd forgotten were stuffed in my ears to protect them from the cannon fire. Oops.

"I said, that was amazing," Joe repeated. "It really felt like I was there."

I rubbed my ears. They were still ringing a little even after using the earplugs.

"Told you," I said with a grin. "Keep listening to me and we might be able to stop your brain from atrophying after all."

"I think I liked you better when you couldn't hear," he quipped, stuffing the earplugs back in my ears as we both laughed.

"Hey, guys," Jen Griffin called out from behind us, and I could have sworn I saw Joe blush. That was a new one. He was usually the smooth one when it came to talking to girls.

"Oh, hey, Jen," Joe said, turning around as she and her friend Daphne walked up with their long Colonial-style dresses swishing over their ankles.

Yup, that was a blush. Jen must have really gotten to him, but she had a way of doing that, what with her combination of girl-next-door prettiness and the kind of unassuming sweetness that made everyone she talked to feel like they were special. Her friend Daphne was pretty cute too, not that she paid much attention to me. Dating was one subject where Joe always scored a lot higher than I did. Apparently, girls don't really appreciate detailed discourses on the origins of forensic anthropology or the ramifications of Southern trade route disruptions prior to the Second Continental Congress. Oh well.

"Hey, Frank," Jen said, being nice and making a point

to include me. Daphne, on the other hand, just raised an indifferent eyebrow and busied herself examining her freshly painted fingernails.

"Hey, Jen, Daphne. So what did you guys think of the reenactment?" I asked, trying to pick up Joe's uncharacteristic conversational slack.

"It was really cool. It felt like we were watching the real thing," Jen said, looking at Joe.

"Hey, that's what we were just saying, right, Joe?" I prodded my brother.

"Um, yeah," he mumbled. Oh man, he had it bad.

"We've got to get over to the *Resolve*," Jen said. "Daphne and I are playing soldiers' wives greeting the ship."

Daphne's mom was on the city council, and she had been pretty involved helping out with the reenactment.

"Okay, cool," I said. "We'll see you guys over there."

"Maybe we can all go out to the diner after," Jen suggested, looking at Joe in a way that made it clear the invitation was meant mostly for him.

I subtly elbowed Joe, who still hadn't untied his tongue. "Um, yeah, that would be really great," he said, rather lamely in my opinion, but at least it was better than a blank stare. Jen smiled and started to leave before turning back to Joe.

"I really like your hat," she said playfully. "I think it looks cute on you."

Joe grinned. The compliment seemed to miraculously revive his confidence.

"And you look like the loveliest girl in all the king's colonies," he replied in what I think he meant to sound like a James Bond accent.

Sure, it was corny and the accent was terrible, but it got a big giggle out of Jen. It was good to see Joe regain his form.

"Till we meet again, milady," he said, then removed the silly red tricorn hat and swept it forward, bowing dramatically.

Jen curtsied in her Colonial dress, her eyes crinkling with a smile, and walked off laughing with Daphne, who, of course, didn't bother to say good-bye. That was okay. I knew Joe really liked Jen, so I didn't mind taking one for the team and being his wingman on a dubious double date with Daphne that night. That didn't mean I couldn't give him a hard time now, though.

"Your British accent is almost as bad as the Don's," I said, which reminded me, "What's up with your general anyway? The Don really seems to be getting into the reenactment."

Now that the smoke had cleared, all the "wounded" soldiers had gotten up, brushed themselves off, and joined the celebration. All of them except Don Sterling. The Don hadn't budged. The battle was over and he was still playing dead on the other side of the field. He seemed to be taking the whole thing very seriously.

"Yeah, he still hasn't broken character. That's some impressive method acting." Joe laughed.

"For the Don, at least," I added.

"He's a regular Don-iel Day-Lewis," Joe cracked, and I

groaned. Some of my brother's jokes are better than others.

"Wow, he really went all out, he even used squibs," Joe observed, referring to the exploding blood packs they use in movies to simulate gunshot wounds. Sure enough, a dark circle had appeared over his chest.

"Mr. Lakin isn't going to be thrilled about him ruining one of the museum's best uniforms," I said, and as if on cue, Mr. Lakin walked up.

"Greetings, boys. I'd say our little reenactment was quite a success," he proclaimed.

"That was some fancy riding, Mr. Lakin," Joe said, barely containing a sly smile. Joe was a pro at tweaking teachers without them knowing it, but Mr. Lakin was onto him. It's a good thing the reenactment had General Lakin in a good mood.

"Ha!" he laughed. "I nearly broke my neck. We would have had to add a new chapter to the history book about the bumbling American general who fell off his horse mid-battle. I think I'm going to be sore for a week."

Mr. Lakin rubbed his backside, getting a good laugh out of Joe and me. Victory had our hardest teacher in a light mood.

"Speaking of rewriting history," he said, and turned his attention to Don Sterling, who was still lying on his side, apparently reveling in his unscripted role as a fallen British general.

"Get up and stop showing off, Don," Mr. Lakin called out. "We've got to get over to the ship for the dedication."

Mr. Lakin made his way over to Don Sterling. "It's bad enough we have to suffer through your performances onstage. Now come on, we're going to be late for our own party. The whole world doesn't stop for you, you know."

Mr. Lakin gave the Don's boot a kick. The Don didn't move.

Joe and I exchanged a glance. Something was definitely not right. Joe knelt down and put his fingers on Don Sterling's neck like we'd been taught in our first aid course.

"I don't think he's acting," Joe said after a moment. "It's hard to fake not having a pulse."

THE DEAD DON

4

JOE

AND JUST LIKE THAT, THE MAKE-BELIEVE battlefield turned into a real crime scene.

"Oh my God, he had a heart attack," someone yelled, and people started to panic.

Mr. Lakin, used to managing disorderly assemblies as a high school teacher, quickly started trying to calm down the onlookers. Another one of the redcoats was an off-duty paramedic, but it was already too late. The Don was gone.

Thankfully, most of the reenactors and the crowd had already headed over to the *Resolve* for the ship's rededication, so the scene was less chaotic than it could have been.

Frank and I have a kind of silent shorthand, and we can usually read each other's thoughts pretty well, which comes in handy at times like this. We looked at each other, and I could tell we were thinking the same thing. A heart attack during the reenactment may have seemed like a logical conclusion. With all the noise and excitement of the reenacted battle, it followed that his heart could have stopped and no one would have noticed until it was too late. Or . . . I looked down at the red blotch on Sterling's shirt above his heart where his coat had fallen open, the one I had first assumed came from a stuntman's trick blood pack. Frank and I exchanged another look.

"It's not a squib," he said in a hushed voice.

"It's a bullet wound," I finished the thought.

"Or a musket ball wound," Frank amended.

Frank pulled out a pen and used it to gently lift the lapel of the Don's red coat so as not to contaminate any evidence. (Leave it to Frank to always carry a pen even while dressed as an eighteenth-century soldier.) Sure enough, there was a hole the size of a .75 caliber musket ball in the fabric above the Don's heart. Don Sterling's unscripted collapse from enemy fire hadn't been an act, and it hadn't been a heart attack or any other natural cause. Someone had really shot the Don through the heart!

The shock of it ricocheted around inside my brain, jolting me straight into detective mode. Where had the shot come from? It definitely seemed like a musket ball had caused the entry wound and not a smaller modern bullet. That meant the shooter was probably one of the reenactors. It was too early to know anything for sure, but it looked like someone had used the reenactment to disguise Don Sterling's murder. It was hard to imagine anyone could be that devious, but . . .

Frank and I whispered to each other so we wouldn't alarm the crowd.

"Someone shot him right in public during the battle without anyone even knowing," I said in amazement.

"If it was one of the soldiers, they wouldn't have even needed a disguise." Frank sounded just as stunned by the audacity of it as I was.

"You're right. With so many muskets going off at the same time, no one would have been able to tell that one of them wasn't firing blanks," I concurred.

Frank nodded gravely. "Not until it was already too late."

"There must have been more than a hundred shots fired. It's going to be a nightmare to even begin trying to figure out which gun fired the real one," I said, unable to hide my frustration.

Frank wrinkled his forehead as he considered the dilemma. "The Don was shot in the chest, so it had to have been someone shooting at him from the American side, right?"

That narrowed down the list. Not that it did us much good. We were still left with a whole regiment full of suspects!

"But who? It could have been any of them," I said.

"It's pretty brilliant, really," Frank said begrudgingly as he began to break down the killer's possible thought process.

"Someone could have hidden in plain sight along with all the other Colonial soldiers and secretly loaded their gun with live ammunition. The killer would have guessed that when the Don collapsed, everyone would think it was just part of the reenactment."

"They guessed right. He even fooled us," I admitted. We'd been duped along with the rest of the town. It felt like being on the receiving end of a cruel prank. I was mad. Frank was too.

"It's murder by reenactment, " he said with disgust.

Murder by reenactment. The killer must have thought he was pretty smart. With so many muskets going off, there was no way to tell which reenactor had fired the live round. Someone had shot one of the town's most prominent residents with the entire town watching and walked away without anybody knowing. It was pretty much the perfect crime.

Or it would be if they got away with it. Frank and I had learned a long time ago not to underestimate your adversary in our line of business, but I had to admit, I was particularly impressed with our perp so far, whoever he was.

As soon as I realized I'd already thought of the killer as "our perp," I knew Frank and I had just found our next case. I looked at Frank. He knew it too. Unfortunately, so did Chief Olaf.

"Don't even think about it, Hardys," his voice boomed.

As Bayport's top cop, Chief Olaf was well acquainted with our extracurricular detective work, and I think he saw us as a fairly routine thorn in his ample side. We've discovered that the police usually like to think they're the ones doing their own jobs. Mostly, I think the chief is jealous that we've caught more criminals in Bayport than he has.

"Did either of you see who shot him?" he asked, already knowing the answer.

"No, Chief," I replied. "It could have been anyone in a militia uniform who fired a gun."

"Well then, as much as I might like to see the Hardy boys locked up and out of my hair, neither of you are suspects, seeing as you're wearing red"—Chief Olaf pointed to my British infantry coat and then to Frank—"and Mr. Sterling obviously wasn't killed by a cannon. That means you are free to go. And by free to go, I mean please leave immediately and get away from my crime scene as fast as your nosy feet will carry you."

"But—" Frank tried to object but didn't get far.

"That's a direct order, Hardys!" Sometimes even the chief gets a little confused and treats us more like disobedient deputies than civilians. He likes to give us a hard time, but mostly he's all hot air. He's always treated us fairly, and I figure he even secretly likes us, at least when we aren't annoying him too much. He just sighed when he saw us lingering around with the crowd that had formed a little farther away from poor Don Sterling's body.

He tried to ignore Frank and me while he shouted out orders to his officers. "Get on down to the ship and bring back everyone in a reenactor uniform, and keep everyone else down there on the dock as potential witnesses. Somebody must have seen something."

Mr. Lakin looked stricken. "Now hold on a second, Chief. Can't all that wait? We've got practically the whole town and guests from as far away as London down there, waiting for us to open the museum. This is a monumental event in Bayport history!"

"So is murder," Chief Olaf replied grimly. "I appreciate how much the museum means to you, Rollie, but the festivities will have to wait. I know you and Don weren't exactly the best of friends, but have some respect for the man. A person has been killed. A person, I might add, just about everyone in town has seen you arguing with lately."

"Are you implying that I'm a suspect?" Mr. Lakin sounded genuinely shocked. "That's outrageous, Chief."

Now this was getting interesting. Of course Mr. Lakin would have to be a suspect, but I don't think Frank and I really wanted to face the fact that one of our favorite teachers might really be capable of murder.

"Now, I don't mean to single you out, Rollie, I'm just pointing out the obvious," the chief told him. "So far as I'm concerned, everyone in a Colonial costume who fired a gun is a suspect. I have to look at every possibility, and a few hundred people just saw you galloping at Don, shooting off your pistol like you were Buffalo Bill."

"Excuse me, Chief," Frank interrupted. "Buffalo Bill Cody wasn't born until the mid-1800s, so he couldn't have been present at a Revolutionary War battle. Paul Revere would be a more fitting reference, since he's famous for riding a horse to let everyone know the British were coming, although I don't recall him also being known as a gunman."

Sometimes Frank can't help himself when it comes to correcting historical discrepancies. Mr. Lakin nodded proudly.

"Well spoken, Frank," our teacher said, taking a break from his indignation at being called a murder suspect to praise his star pupil. I don't think Chief Olaf held Frank's devotion to historical accuracy in quite the same esteem. If eyes could shoot laser beams, his would have. He took a deep breath and had to collect himself to keep from yelling.

"Joe, please get your brother out of here before I arrest him for provoking an officer." Chief Olaf took another deep breath and turned to Frank. "You're volunteering at the museum, right? Well, make yourselves useful and get down there to help them close up shop. Everything on that ship is potential evidence, and I don't want a bunch of people wandering around mucking it up."

"Yes, sir!" we both said in unison, seeing our chance to escape the chief's wrath and carry on our investigation without directly antagonizing him. He sighed again. I think he realized his mistake.

"And no snooping!" he yelled after us as we left the park.

Behind us, we could hear Mr. Lakin protesting to the chief. Our history teacher seemed a lot more concerned with the delay to the museum's opening than Don Sterling's murder.

BRITISH INVASION

5

FRANK

WE'D BARELY MADE IT OUT OF THE park when we were intercepted by a tall, slim man in a pin-striped suit hurrying up the path.

"Excuse me, but judging by your uniforms, I'm guessing you gents know the lay of the land around here," he said in a crisp British accent, a real one. "Do you happen to know where I might find Mr. Sterling?"

That was an odd question. Word about the murder definitely would have been all over the dock by now. Either he somehow hadn't heard or he was hoping to catch a glimpse of the Don's corpse.

"Mr. Sterling is still up at the park," Joe said, trying to puzzle out what the odd stranger with the accent wanted.

With the Don dead, any new information we could gather might help us figure out who wanted him that way and why.

"Splendid. Can you point me in the right direction?" The man glanced down at a gold watch that probably cost more than my dad's car. "My flight from Heathrow was delayed. I've just now arrived, and I had hoped to speak with him as soon as possible."

"The park is up there"—Joe pointed back the way we'd come—"but I don't think Mr. Sterling is going to be doing much speaking."

"Now see here, young man," he snapped, "I can assure you Mr. Sterling will, in fact, be very eager to hear what I have to say."

"Um, what my brother means to say is that Mr. Sterling won't be speaking to anyone. He, uh, died unexpectedly during the reenactment." I figured it was up to the police to decide what they wanted to tell the public about the murder, and I didn't want to divulge too much anyway until we knew what our friend from England wanted with the Don.

"Dead, you say? What a shame. I'd very much hoped to speak with him, and it's a rather long way to travel to find the man you're supposed to meet with is deceased."

The man didn't seem all that concerned with the circumstances of the Don's death, just the inconvenience it caused him. This was getting to be a trend.

"Do you know, by chance, who else I might be able to speak with about some of the, uh, items recovered during the ship's restoration?" he asked, drawing his eyebrows into a kind of question mark.

"Mr. Lakin is running the museum, but I don't think there's going to be much museum business going on, not today at least," I said, thinking about how upset Mr. Lakin had been when Chief Olaf put the kibosh on the opening.

"If you see this Mr. Lakin, please inform him that I'd like to seek an audience with him posthaste." He handed me a gold-embossed business card with the name DIRK BISHOP and the words ANTIQUES & ANTIQUITIES.

"Any specific message you'd like us to relay when we see him?" Joe went fishing for more information, but Dirk Bishop didn't take the bait.

Bishop looked down at Joe's private's uniform dismissively. "No. I'd say these matters are above your rank."

He turned abruptly and started walking up the path to the park. After a few steps, he stopped to look back over his shoulder at the USS *Resolve* docked in the harbor below.

"Rather a shame, indeed. I had so hoped to speak with Mr. Sterling," he mumbled absently to himself before continuing on his way.

"Well, I guess that's our Londoner," Joe said after he was gone and we'd started walking back down the hill to the harbor.

"Strange guy," I observed.

"Rude dude too," Joe added.

"Him showing up from England right after the Don's

death could be a coincidence or it could be connected some-how. We'll have to keep an eye on him, see if we can find out what he wants to talk about with Mr. Lakin," I told Joe.

"Speaking of Mr. Lakin . . . ," Joe began.

"I know," I said wearily. "He has to be a suspect, but I just can't believe Mr. Lakin would do it."

I knew where Joe was going with this, and I didn't like thinking about one of my favorite teachers maybe also being a murderer. I hoped we could prove otherwise, but I wasn't going to let my feelings compromise our investigation either way. I was going to follow the evidence wherever it led, even if it led back to Mr. Lakin.

"I don't like it either, but we have to consider the possi-bility," Joe told me. "Chief Olaf is right; their beef gave him a motive, and everyone saw him charge at the Don, firing his pistol right about the same time the Don was shot for real. We can't eliminate him as a suspect."

We were quiet for a minute, letting the information sink in while we made our way through the harbor toward the *Resolve*. I wondered if Mr. Lakin really hated Don Sterling enough to kill him. And could he really be brazen enough to gun a man down in cold blood with the whole town watching? It was hard to imagine. Not just because he was my history teacher, but it would take a pretty good shot to hit a mov-ing target from a galloping horse. Then again, Mr. Lakin had already displayed hidden talents by even riding a horse in the first place, although he had almost fallen off in the process.

Joe echoed my thoughts. "I'm not convinced Mr. Lakin could make that shot even if he wanted to. I think he'd be too smart to take such a difficult shot from horseback and risk missing the Don and hitting someone else. So either Mr. Lakin is secretly an expert marksman or I don't think he's our shooter."

I hoped Joe was right.

"Well, right now it looks like he's the chief's number one suspect," I said.

We both knew Chief Olaf had been wrong before.

"So who else wanted Don Sterling dead?" Joe asked the obvious question we'd need to answer to solve the crime.

At the start of a new mystery, Joe and I like to review the facts, figure out what we know, what we don't, and who to look at to start filling in the blanks. Some cases were pretty straightforward. This wasn't one of them.

"Besides half of Bayport? It's not hard to find people around here with motive," I replied. "Don Sterling wasn't exactly citizen of the year."

"Well, we know who had the means and the opportunity, but that doesn't help us much, since it includes just about everyone on the American side of the reenactment," Joe observed glumly. "At least half of them probably have reason to hate Don Sterling. Mr. Carr and the rest of the Bayport Players actors couldn't stand him. Pete Carson and Rob Hernandez both lost their jobs when he shipped the furniture factory overseas, and Amir Kahn and a bunch of other Bayport High kids had parents who did too."

"I don't know the details, but there was also that thing with Mr. Griffin attacking the Don last year after the factory closed. I think he was arrested or something. So even Mikey could have had a motive," I said reluctantly, knowing Joe wouldn't be happy about possibly having to investigate Jen's brother.

"Great," he huffed. "That should really help my cause with Jen."

"For all we know, it could have been any of them. So how do we figure out which one of those guns fired a real shot? Using a musket was a stroke of genius. Ballistic fingerprinting on smoothbore muzzle loaders is almost impossible," I told Joe, thankful that the online course in forensic ballistics I'd taken from the criminology college had finally come in handy.

Unfortunately, the news wasn't good. A lot of times, police forensics experts can use a gun's "fingerprint" to match a bullet back to the gun that fired it by looking at the unique markings the gun's barrel leaves on the bullet once it's recovered. But the old muskets from the reenactment had "smoothbore" barrels. That means they're basically just a smooth metal pipe on the inside without the "rifling"— the spiraled grooves inside the barrels of modern guns that were invented after the Revolutionary War to make the bullet spin so it flies straighter. A smooth barrel is kind of like a thumb without a print.

Joe sighed. "And even if a lab gets lucky and somehow

figures it out, the chief would still have to send every gun that was fired to New York, and that could take months. And that's only part of the problem. Even if we know which gun fired the shot, how do we figure out which soldier fired that gun? There must have been fifty identical muskets fired, and they all look the same. Bernie collected them all after the reenactment and piled them all together. Just matching the guns back up to their shooters could be as hard as figuring out which one fired the shot."

"Unless we get lucky with a print or DNA," I said.

A second later it hit us.

"Bernie!" we both said in unison.

"We have to get down to the museum before he accidentally messes up the evidence without even knowing it," Joe exclaimed.

"Once he cleans the guns and puts them away with the rest of the ship's muskets, we won't even be able to tell which ones were used in the reenactment, let alone who used them," I called back to Joe as we started running toward the *Resolve*.

We pushed our way through the crowd that had gathered on the dock as quickly as we could without throwing people to the ground. Chief Olaf must have radioed to tell the officers we were coming, because they let us right through the police barrier onto the *Resolve*.

It was hard to really appreciate while rushing up the gangplank, but the *Resolve* was an impressive vessel. At 140 feet long, with three towering masts and ten big cannons poking out of gun ports along either side of the black-and-gold hull, it definitely stood out in a modern harbor full of fishing boats, small yachts, and water taxis.

The deck of the ship was like an awesome interactive outdoor museum, where visitors could explore and learn how the ship sailed. Most of the museum's exhibits were inside on the lower decks. The galley, the captain's cabin, the berth deck where the crew slept, the gun deck where the cannons were, and a bunch of other parts of the enormous ship had all been restored, with different exhibits built into them, displaying all the things they'd found in the crates.

If we were lucky, one of those exhibits would contain the murder weapon. That's the one we wanted, and our destination would turn out to be every bit as dangerous as it sounded.

We were headed for the armory.

BELOW DECK 6

JOE

S O YEAH, RUNNING THROUGH THE EMPTY ship was pretty eerie. Frank knew his way around the *Resolve* really well by now, so I let him lead the way down into the big frigate, where the gun deck was. I'd heard rumors that the ship was haunted by the Colonial sailors who died on it when it was attacked. Not that I believed it or anything, but . . .

Well, all empty like that, with the clomping of our boots on the old wood floor echoing around us like we were trapped inside a giant barrel and the smell of black powder still in the air from the cannon fire, it was easy to imagine we were being chased through a ghost ship. I tried not to think too much about it as I followed Frank past the rows of cannons toward the armory, where they kept the displays with the guns and ammunition.

As we got closer, we could hear what sounded like Bernie humming some kind of tune from inside the armory. I think it might have been classical music, which was weird, because Bernie is this big, tough, action-hero-looking guy.

"Hey, Bernie, it's Frank Hardy!" my brother called out. "We need to talk to you!"

There wasn't any response. When we ran into the armory, we saw why—Bernie sat on top of a crate with his headphones on, calmly cleaning one of the muskets with expert speed and precision while humming along to music so loud you could hear it blaring out from inside his ears. The guy had to be half deaf already to listen to music that loudly without his ears bleeding. No wonder he couldn't hear us. I guessed our gun safety instructor hadn't followed his own advice about wearing earplugs when you shoot to protect your hearing.

"Bernie!" Frank yelled again, but Bernie didn't even notice we were there.

He went right ahead with the next musket, obliviously obliterating any trace of forensic evidence as he wiped it down with an oily cloth, ran a fluffy white rod down the barrel, and added it to the racks of pristine muskets that lined the walls behind the open glass case. He'd already cleaned over half the guns. As hard as it might have been to identify the murder weapon before, this could make it impossible.

We hollered like crazy for Bernie to stop. The room was a lot smaller than the gun deck but still pretty big, and it seemed like there were enough muskets and other weapons in it to equip a small army. We ran across it screaming Bernie's name, but he might as well have been inside a soundproof bubble.

Frank reached out to tap his shoulder and get his attention. Big mistake.

The instant Frank's hand touched his shoulder, *WHAM*. In a flash, Bernie had Frank slammed up against the wall with his feet dangling off the floor. It was like someone had surprised a very large, very angry viper. He had struck so fast, neither of us had time to react. Now, I'm a green belt in tae kwon do and I'd like to think I'm pretty quick, but this guy moved like a real professional warrior. Which made sense considering the large Marine Corps logo on his bulging forearm. I'd forgotten that Bernie had gotten the job because of his experience as an armorer while serving in the Special Forces. His military background was hard not to notice now that Frank's unexpected tap on the shoulder had sent him into full-on soldier mode. This was one guy you didn't want to accidentally surprise in a roomful of weapons.

"Bernie, no! It's just Frank!" I yelled as loud as I could, hoping my voice would penetrate the wall of music being pumped directly into his brain by his headphones. It had been a lot funnier when it was just Frank forgetting to take out his earplugs after the reenactment.

It may have felt like forever, but the whole thing really only lasted a second before Bernie realized who it was and dropped Frank like he was a hot potato.

"Frank Hardy?" he asked with a bewildered look on his face.

"Graackafrack!" Frank sputtered.

"What are you doing in here?" Bernie said in confusion. "Are you crazy, running up behind an armed man like that?"

Frank muttered something that sounded like a cross between an apology and a whimper. I don't think he was really hurt, just too shocked to respond coherently.

"I could have killed you." Bernie sounded horrified. And angry, too. "Didn't you learn anything from the firearm safety class? If we had been using live ammunition today, you could have been accidentally shot!"

"But someone did use live ammunition," I told him. "That's why we're here. Don Sterling was shot."

Frank nodded. "And it wasn't an accident."

Bernie furrowed his brow and grunted. He's usually the strong, silent type. That and a stern look of concentration were about as much reaction as we got out of him for the next few minutes. I translated his grunt as, *What are you talking about? Tell me more.* So we filled him in on the Don's murder and needing to preserve the guns as evidence for the police.

Bernie looked down at the stack of uncleaned guns like they were a difficult puzzle he didn't know the answer to.

"Bernie, do you know how someone might have really

loaded one of the muskets after you brought them to the reenactment? Did you see anything?" I asked.

"Hardys!" Chief Olaf bellowed from the armory doorway.

It looked like we were going to have to wait to get any useful information out of Bernie.

"This might sound like a dumb question, but why are you questioning my witness?" the chief wanted to know.

"We were on our way here to help close up the museum, Chief, just like you asked, when we realized Bernie might not know to put the guns aside as evidence and not clean them," I tried to explain.

"As you can see, I am perfectly capable of coming to that realization on my own," Chief Olaf retorted defensively. "It is my job, after all."

"Yes, sir, but we just realized it quicker." I pointed out the stack of uncompromised guns we'd managed to save by acting fast.

In retrospect, that probably wasn't the best idea. The chief shut his eyes tightly and took a deep breath. I think he was counting to three to try to calm down. I can have that effect on him. When he opened his eyes again, he said, "I don't know which of you boys I don't like more."

The chief gave Frank a long look. "You okay, Frank? You're paler than usual."

He really was. I still don't think my brother had gotten over the shock of Bernie attacking him like that.

Frank threw me a look that said, *Do we tell him?* He was

struggling with the same thing I was—would it do any good to get Bernie in trouble for assaulting Frank? I wanted to give Bernie the benefit of the doubt. I actually really liked the guy. He had that cool commando thing going, and all the kids in the gun safety class were kind of scared of him and looked up to him at the same time. Besides, Frank hadn't gotten hurt, and I don't think either of us wanted to get further on Bernie's bad side, especially if we hoped to get information out of him.

The chief's antenna must have gone up when Frank didn't answer right away. "What's going on here?" he demanded.

Bernie saved us the trouble and came clean on his own.

"He took me by surprise," he said, absently rubbing the Marine Corps tattoo on his forearm. "Frank came up behind me while I was cleaning the guns and caught me off guard. I thought I was being attacked. I acted on instinct and put a defensive move on him before I realized who it was." Bernie sounded ashamed of himself.

"You're telling me you mistook Frank Hardy for a threat?" The chief smirked. It was pretty funny when you thought about it. Frank is in decent shape, but he isn't exactly intimidating, and next to Bernie he looked about as threatening as a toddler. I don't think either Frank or Bernie saw the humor in it.

"I wouldn't have really hurt him," Bernie said defensively. "And he should have known better than to sneak up on a man while he's handling weapons. You do that to a man in combat, and chances are you won't be around anymore to learn your lesson."

"Lucky for us we aren't in combat," the chief said, giving Bernie a weary look. "Frank? That what happened?"

"It was really stupid of me, Chief," Frank admitted. "He couldn't hear me because of his headphones, and I shouldn't have surprised him like that while he was cleaning a gun. Bernie is right. It's poor gun safety, and I should have known better."

I could tell Frank really did feel bad about not being more careful. I think he felt kind of like he'd failed an exam. It's not often you can get Frank Hardy to admit he's stupid about anything.

"You're right, Frank, that was stupid of you," the chief said, before turning to Bernie and adding, "But you should know better than to let yourself be distracted by music while handling firearms."

"Yes, sir." Bernie snapped to attention like he was being dressed down by a superior officer. "It won't happen again."

The chief sighed (he does that a lot around us) and turned back to Frank and me. "Why is it whenever there's trouble around here, you two always seem to be in the middle of it?"

"In our defense, Chief, we did save a lot of evidence from being ruined," I reminded him.

"That was a rhetorical question, Joe." Chief Olaf sighed again. "But you're right. And to thank you, I'm going to allow you to leave the boat without arresting you both for interfering with a police investigation."

"It's actually—" Frank started, but the chief stopped him.

"Yes, Frank, I know, the *Resolve* is technically a ship and not a boat. Now go!" He sounded totally exasperated, not that I really blame him; Frank doesn't always have the best timing.

"Yes, sir," we both said, and turned to leave.

"Your 'Get Out of Jail Free' cards expire in one minute," he called after us. "If I catch either of you anywhere near this ship before this investigation wraps, I'm taking you in."

We hadn't even made it to the door yet when we heard a loud clatter behind us. I turned around just in time to see Bernie trip and knock a large tin of gun solvent all over the pile of uncleaned guns.

For an awful moment the only sound in the armory was the glug-glug-glugging of spilled oil, washing away whatever was left of the evidence.

OFF-LIMITS 7

FRANK

EVIDENCE I'D NEARLY GOTTEN KILLED trying to protect!

Bernie looked mortified as he fumbled to recover the tin canister and put the cap back on, but the damage had already been done. Oil had soaked the flintlocks and trigger guards of a lot of the remaining muskets. If there was trace evidence that might help us link the muskets back to the shooters, there was a good chance that's where it would be. Or would have been if Bernie hadn't poured oil all over it.

"I'm sorry, sir, I'll take care of it," Bernie stammered, and hastily started trying to soak up the spilled solvent with a rag. He sounded so embarrassed I almost couldn't help feeling a little bad for him.

"Leave it, Bernie," Chief Olaf ordered. "You've done enough already."

"But—" Bernie started to protest.

"We'll take it from here," the chief cut him off. "This is police evidence now, what's left of it at least."

"But if I don't wipe up the excess solvent, it could stain the guns," Bernie pleaded. "I could lose my job."

"I'm sorry, Bernie." Chief Olaf sounded like he really was; police chiefs can be nice guys too. "We'll do our best to take good care of the guns while we have them, and I'll talk to Rollie and make sure he goes easy on you," he continued. "Mistakes happen, and we're all under a lot of pressure here with this Sterling situation."

"Yes, sir," Bernie said.

Chief Olaf looked over at us and said, "I thought I told you two to get!" For once, I was relieved to be chased off by the police.

"Bernie Blank is kind of a scary guy," Joe said to me once we were out of earshot.

"You think?" I asked him. My voice came out all hushed. Bernie's attack had only lasted a moment, but it had left me shaken.

"I'm guessing that was one of those rhetorical questions the chief was talking about," Joe said. I think he meant to lighten the mood, but I wasn't really up for laughing.

You play detective long enough and you're going to get in a few fights. We never look for them—and we always try to defuse them with words before resorting to fists—but the Hardy boys won't back down if it means defending ourselves or helping someone in trouble. I may not be that big, but I'm scrappy, and with Joe and I having each other's backs, I usually like our chances. Back in the armory? I didn't have a shot. Zilch. Zip. Zero. As in the Big Zero. Zero-days-left-on-this-planet-Zero. It's not like I saw my life flash before my eyes or anything super dramatic like that, but it really is frightening being cornered with no control over what happens to you next.

I didn't know whether to be angry at Bernie, though. I had come up behind him in a roomful of expensive guns, after all. It's possible any veteran soldier in that situation might have reacted the same way to a perceived threat. He was obviously also a little unstable. That didn't necessary mean he had nefarious purposes.

In a mystery like this, you have to question everyone's motives, but there's a thin line between healthy investigative suspicion and paranoia. But then again, as Joe likes to misquote, "Just because you're paranoid doesn't mean they aren't actually trying to eat your brains."

"It's kind of hard for me to be objective about Bernie after the dude nearly ripped my head off," I admitted.

"I'm not too happy with the guy either, but just because he's a terrifying super soldier with a screw loose doesn't mean he's guilty of anything." Joe spoke the truth. Being scary isn't a crime.

"I guess," I conceded. "He didn't actually end up hurting me, and he sure could have if he'd wanted to."

We went back and forth about it, trying on ideas. It helps to have two people to bounce things around like that. You're able to get a fresher perspective. It's one of the many benefits of having a good partner in crime (or in our case, crime solving).

"But why would he want to hurt you in the first place?" Joe continued to make his point. "It's not like him cleaning the guns was suspicious. He was just doing his job."

That much was true, but . . .

"Was he still just doing his job when he spilled solvent all over the guns he hadn't cleaned yet? Sure, it was probably just an accident, but it was a pretty convenient accident for whoever does benefit from the evidence being compromised," I said, reminding us just how difficult it was going to be to figure which gun was which with most of them wiped clean.

"It looks funny, yeah, but what reason would he have for destroying the evidence, especially if he didn't even know it was evidence? He would have been back at the ship with his headphones on before news ever reached the dock about the Don. He wouldn't have heard until we told him."

"Unless he knew already," I said, but it didn't fit.

As far as I knew, Bernie hadn't even shot a gun at the reenactment, which made him a pretty unlikely assassin. He had been dressed as a Colonial officer and had been wearing a pistol and a saber like the rest of the officers, but he'd only been supervising.

"Yeah, it's a stretch. He certainly has the qualifications to be the shooter if he had a mind to, but it's hard to shoot someone without firing a gun," I said, frustrated at finding ourselves at an another dead-end line of inquiry.

"He sure was slick handling those guns, though," Joe said admiringly.

"And handling me," I added reluctantly.

"The guy was like a ninja commando," Joe continued. "He must have been pretty flustered to mess up like that with the solvent."

"I guess even terrifying super soldiers get a case of the nerves sometimes. Who wouldn't be shaken up by accidentally almost killing a kid, getting yelled at by the chief of police, and maybe losing their job?" I said. It felt strange defending the guy who had just attacked me, but Bernie had always been nice to me before, and until a few minutes ago, he'd been one of my favorite members of the museum staff.

Joe cut to the chase. "Even if he had a fired a gun, it wouldn't make any sense without a motive anyway. Sure, the Don probably wasn't the best boss, but he still signed the checks Bernie cashed every two weeks, right? You don't take out the guy who pays your bills."

"Don Sterling's death puts the whole museum in jeopardy. Bernie could end up out of a job, and you saw how worried he was about that already," I said, thinking Bernie had a lot more reason to want the Don alive than dead.

Joe was right: Everything Bernie had done had an innocent explanation. Even if he had acted suspiciously, he still wasn't anything more than a person of interest. Without a means or a motive, he wasn't our shooter. Which left us right back where we started.

We'd been taking our time leaving, kind of just wandering while we talked out what had happened in the armory. I hadn't realized how far into the ship we were. Part of the museum was still under construction, and we were in one of the last completed exhibits before everything was roped off.

This room had one of my favorite displays. It was a small one—just one case with a plaque, some illustrations, and a single gold coin—but it was one of the coolest. It was about an old local legend of lost British gold that had supposedly been seized by the Continental Army around the same time as the Battle of Bayport. Every kid in Bayport had heard about the legend of the "King's Pride Treasure." When we were little, Joe and I used to run around the docks pretending we were treasure hunters on the run from pirates. Of course, we never found anything. That didn't mean that no one else had, and it was fun to think it still might be out there somewhere. The gold coin in the display was just a replica of the kind of coin that would have been sent from England to help fund the war. It wasn't even real gold. In a weird way, though, seeing it made me feel like a kid again.

I let my imagination run wild for a minute before Joe's voice snapped me back to reality. "Did you hear that?"

I looked up and listened. We weren't alone. I hadn't heard it at first because my hearing was still a little wonky from the reenactment, but the sound of footsteps on the ship's wood floor and muffled voices were getting louder.

"We better skedaddle. The chief is going to blow his top if he catches us still on the ship." I started leading the way back, hoping whoever it was would veer off into one of the corridors before reaching us. Yeah . . . no . . . so much for that one. A staticky voice blurted something over a police radio, and it sounded like the officer carrying it was headed right for us.

"What now, dude?" Joe asked.

Good question. There was no other way I knew of to get out of the museum from that part of the ship, and there wasn't anywhere to hide in the exhibit we were in. . . .

There was, however, the roped-off corridor leading to the part of the museum that was still under construction. It was off-limits to most of the museum's volunteers and employees because of the insurance risk, so I'd never been back there before. I was excited at the prospect of exploring a part of the ship I hadn't seen, although I would have preferred to do it while not running from the police. I eyed the yellow caution tape crisscrossing the entrance.

"This way," I said, and darted past a big yellow sign that read DANGER—DO NOT ENTER.

BEHIND THE SCENES

8

JOE

I REALLY HOPED FRANK KNEW WHAT HE WAS doing. Next to the big DO NOT ENTER sign was another one that said CONSTRUCTION ZONE—HARD HAT REQUIRED BEYOND THIS POINT. I'd been accused of being hardheaded before, but I didn't think that would do me much good when a beam fell on my noggin.

We ducked under the ropes and out of sight a second before the officer stepped into the room. He hadn't seen us! The relief I felt at our narrow escape didn't last long—in the construction zone it got real dark, real quick. There weren't any lights installed yet, and the portals were sealed off, blocking out the sunlight that filtered through most of the ship during the day. In the dark like that . . . Ack, there I go thinking about ghost stories again.

"Ouch!" I exclaimed a little too loudly as I stumbled on a loose board.

"Shhh," Frank reminded me rather unnecessarily.

"Sorry, bro, my X-ray vision is on the fritz," I whispered back.

A second later two small lights illuminated Frank and me. We'd both had the idea to use the flashlights on our phones at the same time.

"Great minds think alike," I said with a smile.

"Come on, Edison," Frank said with a smirk. "Let's find another way out of here."

Frank started leading the way. I was counting on all the time my brother had spent aboard the *Resolve* and at home studying the huge ship's design to get us out of there safely. Sometimes Frank's nerd power comes in handy.

"I hope you know where you're going," I told him.

"So do I," he replied. Well, that was reassuring.

I followed Frank past dangerous-looking construction equipment, jagged nail-toothed boards, and precariously stacked piles of debris. Our flashlights weren't especially strong, but they were a whole lot better than nothing. As creepy as it had been running through the empty ship in the daylight, this felt like some serious haunted-house stuff, with lots of dark corners and crooked shadows. I was more worried about the rickety state of the ship than ghosts, though. Light reflected off yellow caution tape where the floor had caved in, and the wood under our feet creaked constantly.

The possibility of the floor collapsing didn't make me feel good about our predicament.

The space we were in came to an end at a gaping hole in the floor with a ladder poking out of it. Luckily, a narrow corridor branched off to the side of the hole, disappearing into darkness. I went to turn down the corridor and stopped short just in time to keep from bumping into Frank and knocking him into the hole. He'd paused at the edge and was deep in thought as he peered down into the pitch blackness below.

"I think that goes down into the storerooms over the cargo hold," he said. "I've always wanted to see where they found all the crates."

"No way, dude," I said, and meant it. He actually looked disappointed. My brother can be an odd duck sometimes.

"Yeah, you're probably right. We could get lost down there in the dark before we found our way back out," he said, pouting.

I shone my little light down the corridor. "What about that way?"

He thought about it for a second. "I think that may be the lower deck of the officers' quarters, where the restoration crew had temporary offices when they first started working on the ship. If I'm right, there should be a way out up onto the deck."

"Aye, aye, Captain," I said with a salute, and followed him down the corridor.

Thankfully, the floor seemed a little safer here. Farther

down, cabin doors started to appear on either side of the corridor. I held my light up to one of the cabin doors, where a handwritten sign said MUSEUM DIRECTOR. I stopped at that one. Bingo.

"Hey, Frank, you said this is where they had the original offices?" I asked, holding the light up to the door for him to see. Frank stopped, looked at the sign, and smiled.

"So this one would have been Mr. Lakin's, huh?" I asked, happily already knowing the answer. We weren't going to get a better chance to snoop around the office of the police's prime suspect.

Frank turned the knob on the creaky door and held it open for me. "After you, sir," he said.

To call it an office was being generous. The little cabin was so filled with barrels and boxes and all kinds of other nautical debris that the actual workspace amounted to little more than a cluttered cubicle. The desk was nothing but a wood plank thrown on top of two barrels, and from the dust covering everything, it didn't look like anyone had been back here in a while. The only thing left on the desk was a small stack of papers and some paper clips.

"Doesn't look like there's much here," I said, feeling let down as I flipped through some random invoices and a museum display case catalog.

"Oh well, it was worth a shot." Frank turned to go, and I turned to follow when my light glinted off something white in the debris behind the desk.

I moved a couple of small boxes where some loose papers had gotten wedged. They must have fallen there unnoticed when Mr. Lakin relocated offices. The first sheet was a past-due home electricity bill in Mr. Lakin's name. I felt kind of guilty looking at Mr. Lakin's personal stuff and flipped quickly to the next item. It was another past-due bill, and I was about to skip past that one too when I caught a glimpse of the dollar amount at the bottom of the invoice. I did a double take and blinked my eyes a couple of times, but the number didn't change.

"Frank, I think you should see this." I called my brother over, and his mouth dropped open.

$87,000. That was how much money the Lakins owed Bayport Memorial Hospital for ongoing medical treatment of Mae Lakin. I had a vague notion that Mr. Lakin was married, but I hadn't known his wife was sick.

"I don't think I feel right looking at this, Joe," Frank said.

"I know, me either, but it could turn out to be relevant to the case if Mr. Lakin was having money trouble. We don't know what information is going to be important yet. We might even find something that can help clear him," I reasoned with Frank.

He sighed his consent. "What's next?"

I flipped the page. Now, this was strange. It was a letter from the NYPD Pension Fund addressed to Rollie Lawrence Lakin. Frank and I exchanged a curious look. I read the letter aloud in a hushed voice.

Dear Mr. Lakin,

I regret to inform you that your appeal has been denied. Upon further review, it has been determined that your wife's condition is not covered under the disability and pension health plan you received upon leaving the department.

I am truly sorry and wish there was more we could do to help. I understand that you were wounded in the line of duty some years ago, and the New York Police Department and the City of New York are deeply grateful for your heroic service as a member of the mounted police unit.

I stopped reading. You don't ever really think much about your teacher's personal lives. Or even that they have them. They're supposed to be kind of like scholastic vampires, who just climb into big school lockers after the day ends and only come back out to teach when the bell rings the next morning. The idea that they could actually have relationships, life crises, and secret pasts just didn't fit into the equation. It looked like I was going to have to come up with a new equation, though, because there was suddenly a lot about our history teacher that didn't fit. Mr. Lakin's wife was sick, he owed a ton of money for hospital bills that weren't covered by his insurance, and, apparently, before he was a teacher, he had been a policeman. That was the real kicker. You could have told me he'd been an astronaut or a lion tamer or an astronaut lion tamer and I wouldn't have been more shocked.

"Did you know Mr. Lakin used to be a cop?" I asked Frank. From the stunned look on my brother's face, I figured the answer was no.

"I just assumed he'd always been a teacher," he said quietly.

Mr. Lakin was a Bayport High institution. He'd been there for at least thirty years. He'd even taught our dad. It was hard to imagine the old guy in the tacky suit as a young man in a policeman's uniform.

"He wasn't just a police officer, Joe," Frank said reluctantly.

"I know," I said before finishing Frank's thought. "He was a police officer who also rode a horse."

"That would have been where he learned how to ride." Frank started to say more, but stopped.

"He also would have learned how to shoot." I added the part Frank didn't want to. "The reenactment wouldn't have been the first time he fired a gun from horseback."

And just like that, the idea that Mr. Lakin could have hit Don Sterling from a galloping horse with a pistol seemed a lot less crazy.

SCHOOL DAZE

9

FRANK

I WAS PRETTY TIRED BY THE TIME JOE AND I dragged ourselves into school the next morning. We'd made it off the *Resolve* unnoticed, but we weren't any closer to solving the mystery, and I don't think either of us got a lot of sleep that night. Not with everything that went down after the reenactment. We'd witnessed one of the town's most prominent people murdered in front of us during a make-believe Revolutionary War battle, one of our favorite teachers had a shocking secret past and might be the prime suspect, and, oh yeah, I'd almost been pulverized by a gun-wielding commando. You try getting a good night's sleep after that!

Whenever I did fall asleep, I kept having this nightmare that Joe and I were caught high up in the *Resolve*'s tallest mast during a massive thunderstorm. Each time it was the same awful dream. A huge wave would crash against the ship, knocking Joe off the mast. I'd grab him, but he'd start to slip from my hands, and I then I'd wake up not knowing if I saved him or not. Ugh. I was glad it was morning.

It wasn't a big surprise that the whole school was buzzing about Don Sterling's murder. There were all kinds of crazy rumors and conspiracy theories flying around. Mr. Lakin was at the center of a lot of them too. Some people were even saying the police had already arrested him. Mr. Lakin disproved that one himself by walking down the crowded hall right before the first-period bell. It was like somebody hit the mute button on the whole school. Everybody shut up all at once and just stared. Even some of the teachers. There were some hushed whispers and murmuring, and Amir even yelled out, "Good shot!" Mr. Lakin just kept his eyes down and headed straight for his classroom.

More than anything else, it was the revelations we'd discovered in Mr. Lakin's old office aboard the *Resolve* that really had me unsettled. His personal and financial lives were in turmoil, and his service as a mounted policeman meant that it might not have been such an impossible shot for him after all. I didn't know how the pieces fit, but they all looked like part of the same puzzle.

Joe and I were going to have to find a way to subtly question him about Don Sterling's death, and I really wasn't looking forward to it. I usually loved my afternoon AP history class, especially now that we were deep into analysis of the Revolutionary War's expansion from a localized Colonial uprising into a world war involving the Spanish and French. It was my last period of the day, and a lot of times I'd hang out at Mr. Lakin's desk after class, going into more detail about the lesson. Not today. Today we weren't going to be talking about history. I was going to be asking him about some very current events, and I didn't think either of us was going to enjoy it very much.

Time was ticking—most murders that aren't solved in the first forty-eight hours are never solved at all—so Joe and I were going to have to make the most of our investigation, even though we were stuck at school. Mr. Lakin wasn't our only lead inside the halls of Bayport High. The Hardy boys' reputation as amateur detectives is pretty well known around Bayport, and a lot of kids just automatically figured we were on the case. That made it hard to keep a low profile, which is how we normally like to operate. People were peppering us with questions, but we were playing dumb (which is easier for Joe than it is for me) and only worrying about the Bayport High kids who might be relevant to the mystery.

As soon as both Joe and I had a free period, we sat down in the cafeteria to go over our notes and eat some lunch. I opened my case file notebook to the pages labeled "Potential Suspects" and "Possible Material Witnesses," and we started running down the names.

Our hippy-dippy drama teacher Mr. Carr and our troubled

classmate Amir Kahn both made the "Potential Suspects" list. Mr. Carr had played a Colonial officer in the reenactment. He'd been pretty bitter about the Don and his deep pockets beating him out for the lead role in the last Bayport Players stage production. Every kid who'd had a class with him had heard his rant on the capitalistic corruption of artistic integrity in the local theater.

Amir had been an infantryman, and both his parents had lost their jobs when Sterling Industries pulled the plug on the furniture factory. He'd had a really hard time of it since the layoffs, sliding from academic all-American to detention.

Calvin Givens was another classmate who made the list. He hadn't participated in the reenactment, so he wasn't really a suspect, but he did have a distinct dishonor that no one else shared: He was Don Sterling's stepson, making him a "Possible Material Witness" we most definitely had to talk to. We were probably going to have to wait to interview him, though. I doubted we'd see him in school the day after his stepfather's murder.

We'd just gotten started breaking down each person of interest on the list when I noticed Joe's face go slack. I looked up and saw why: Jen and Daphne had just walked in the cafeteria door.

"Oh man, I totally forgot about our date at the diner last night," Joe said, putting his face in his hands.

I had forgotten too, but then again, I had a lot less to lose than Joe did. It's not like Daphne would have missed me. I really wanted things to work out for Joe and Jen, though, so I hoped she would forgive the date flake.

"I'm sure she'll understand," I assured him, hoping I was right. "I think yesterday's plans probably went off the rails for just about everybody after the Don turned up dead."

We were about to find out whether Jen understood. She was headed straight for us. I could sense Joe tensing up next to me. As Jen got closer to our table, she burst into a big smile, and Joe let out a big sigh of relief.

"Hey, Jen," he said, returning her smile with a goofy grin of his own.

"Hey, guys," she said. "We missed you at the diner last night."

"Oh, yeah, well, um, I, it, uh . . . ," Joe fumbled for something to say. I decided to step in to try to save him.

"Things kind of got a little crazy yesterday, you know, with all the excitement after the reenactment," I said, trying not to go into too much detail about the specific nature of our excitement.

"You think we could get a rain check for tonight, maybe?" Jen asked Joe.

Joe smiled. "Definitely. That would be awesome."

"Hey, so everybody is saying that you guys were the ones who discovered the body. Is it true?" Daphne asked me, all excited. She was actually talking to me. That was a first. I guess she wasn't mute after all. The juicy gossip must have cured her.

"You guys are, like, detectives, right? So you're totally investigating the murder, yeah?" Daphne sped right ahead without even waiting for an answer. "Oh my God, that is so cool!"

Okay, so maybe I did have a chance with Daphne after all. Sometimes being an amateur detective has its perks.

Jen didn't seem to share her friend's excitement. At all. Her smile had vanished entirely.

"Why are you even bothering? It's not like anybody really cares that Don Sterling is dead," she said coldly. It was the first time I'd seen Jen Griffin be anything but sweet.

Joe was totally caught off guard too. He actually looked hurt. Joe is a fun-loving guy, but he takes our investigating seriously, and the girl he dug had just dismissed it as a waste of time. This was a side of Jen neither of us had seen before. We had known that something had gone down between Don Sterling and Jen's dad, but we didn't have any of the details. Whatever it was, she obviously didn't have any sympathy for the Don's plight.

"Come on, Daph, let's go. We have study group," she ordered Daphne.

"Oh, um, okay." Daphne seemed just as surprised by her friend's behavior as we were. "We'll see you guys later, yeah? Good luck with the investigation!"

Jen grabbed Daphne by the arm and was about to drag her away when she saw the page on the table labeled "Potential Suspects." I tried to casually close the notebook, but she'd already seen everything she needed to. The fifth name down was Mikey Griffin. Her brother.

"You leave my brother alone!" she yelled at Joe, loud enough that people at some of the other tables looked up to see what was going on. She realized she was causing a scene and flushed with embarrassment. She lowered her voice, trying to keep it calm, but the edge was still there when she started talking again.

"My brother didn't have anything to do with it. If you go around calling him a murderer, he could lose his football scholarship. Sterling already did enough damage to my family when he was alive. Don't you dare let him mess things up more. Leave Mikey out of it. Just stay away from him."

It wasn't a request.

"But, Jen, we—" Joe started to protest.

Jen quickly shut him up. "And you can stay away from me, too, while you're at it."

GRUDGE MATCH

10

JOE

SHELL-SHOCKED. THAT'S ABOUT HOW I felt after Jen reamed me out about our investigation and stormed off like I had just stepped on her favorite puppy.

"I guess that means our date is off for tonight," I said to Frank as I watched Jen drag Daphne behind her out of the cafeteria. Daphne gave us a weak smile and shrugged her shoulders in confusion as the cafeteria doors slammed shut.

"Well, that was . . . unexpected," Frank said with his usual flair for understatement.

A slap in the face would have been unexpected. Jen's sudden outburst felt more like a bombshell. It had simultaneously managed to turn both my love life and our case on their heads. I had been worried about Mikey's name coming up and maybe messing things up with Jen and me—I was used to our detective work getting in the way of my love life for one reason or another—but I hadn't expected this. Jen's reaction to our investigation into the Don's murder was . . . well, suspicious is what it was.

I mean, sure, any girl might be upset if they found out their brother was a murder suspect, but Jen hadn't even given me a chance to explain. She'd just flipped out. And she obviously had a serious grudge against Don Sterling already. She had turned on us as soon as Daphne said we were investigating the murder, before she even saw Mikey's name.

I hoped that it would turn out to be nothing and Jen and I could rewind things and start fresh. I wasn't optimistic, though. I cringed at the thought of adding her name to the "Possible Material Witnesses" list, but the bad blood between the Griffin family and Don Sterling was obvious. Obvious enough that we weren't going to have any choice but to look into it. Our dad taught us that you have to follow the evidence wherever it leads. Sometimes it's a harder lesson to swallow than others. So far, this case was leading Frank and me all kinds of places we didn't really want to go.

"You okay, man? Why do you think she totally lost it?" Frank asked.

I didn't know, but I had a hunch we were about to find out. Someone else had just come through the cafeteria doors, and they were lumbering toward us like they had something they wanted to discuss. Unfortunately, sometimes Mikey Griffin preferred to do the discussing with his fists.

"Uh-oh," Frank said as Mikey made his way across the cafeteria with a scowl on his mean mug and his broad linebacker's shoulders hunched like a gorilla's.

"Do you think Jen would have sicced her brother on us?" I asked Frank in disbelief.

This wouldn't be the first time someone had tried to intimidate us off a case, but until five minutes ago I'd been thinking of Jen Griffin as my future girlfriend. Those warm and fuzzy feelings were starting to get room temperature real quick.

Mikey had the physique, strength, and speed of a top football prospect. Which is exactly what he was. He also had a real short temper when it came to protecting his little sister. In other words, he could be getting ready to do some serious damage. I took some comfort in the fact that he was confronting us without his usual entourage—the entire Bayport High defensive line—there to get his back. He was still going to be a handful all by himself, though, even against the mighty Hardy boys tag team.

It was this kind of situation where our silent shorthand comes in useful. Frank looked at me and I nodded back.

We braced ourselves for a fight. We weren't expecting a confession.

CAFETERIA CONFESSIONAL

11

FRANK

JOE NODDED AT ME, AND WE BOTH ZONED in on Mikey. If he tried anything, I'd go left and Joe would go right, dividing Mikey's attention while keeping the table between us as a barrier to give us extra time to talk some sense into him. Not that Mikey Griffin was known for his good sense.

A few seconds later he stood towering over our table, looking down at us, not saying a word. Joe and I both tensed, hoping it wouldn't come to that, but ready to defend ourselves if we had to. Nothing happened, though. Mikey just stood there looking thuggishly uncomfortable.

Now, Mikey may not be the sharpest bulb in the deck, but he was rarely at a loss for words. The guy usually ran his mouth nonstop. On the field, in the halls, in class, and naturally, in detention. His silence as he stood looming over us was unnerving. It didn't seem like some kind of intimidation tactic, though. It seemed, well, it just seemed awkward. Big, brash Mikey Griffin looked like the one who was intimidated.

"Hey, guys," Mikey finally said without meeting our eyes.

Joe and I exchanged perplexed looks.

"Um, hey, Mikey," I said uncertainly.

"So, like, how's it going?" Mikey asked.

"Uh, it's going okay, Mikey," Joe said, and gave me another confused look. "Is there something we can help you with?"

"So you guys are, like, investigating Mr. Sterling's murder, right?" Mikey asked.

"Um, yeah," Joe replied cautiously. *Here it comes*, I thought, but my gut's natural fight-or-flight instinct didn't seem all that concerned. Something was off. It was really weird that Mikey referred to the Don as Mr. Sterling, for one. He was talking about the guy responsible for ruining his family's lives, according to Jen. What was Mikey's angle?

"Oh, okay, cool," Mikey said, nervously looking over his shoulder like somebody might be spying on him. "Um, do you guys think it would be okay if we, like, talked in private somewhere?"

Joe and I hesitated. If Mikey did want to fight us, following him to some dark corner of the school where there were no witnesses—or easy access to medical attention—was probably a bad idea.

"I'm not sure that's such a good idea," Joe said, trying to be diplomatic.

"Oh, okay. You guys are probably really busy with the investigation and all, huh?" Mikey looked all humbled and started fidgeting. "It's just that Jen would be really mad at me if she saw me talking to you guys. I, uh, I hid until she left the cafeteria so she wouldn't see me."

Now this was getting interesting. Mikey was afraid of his harmless (or so I'd thought until a few minutes ago) little sister. She hadn't sent Mikey after us. He had come to us behind her back. Either that or this was some bizarre ploy to lure us into an ambush. I didn't think Mikey had any intention of strong-arming us, though. The Mikey standing in front of us seemed more like a gentle giant than an ill-willed enforcer, and he didn't sound like a guy who was about to beat us to a pulp. He sounded like a guy who was in trouble and needed our help.

"I was going to tell the police, but Jen wouldn't let me, and she wouldn't want me talking to you about it either, but I had to tell someone and you guys seem cool, so, uh, yeah, but if you don't have time, that's cool too, I guess," Mikey said as he turned to leave, looking rejected. "Sorry for bothering you."

That sealed it. We both jumped up at the same time to stop him from going. Whatever it was Mikey needed help with was something we most definitely needed to hear.

A couple of minutes later the three of us were seated outside on a bench around the corner from the cafeteria.

"So you know about my dad, right?" Mikey asked, and launched into his story without waiting for an answer.

"He was supposed to be promoted at the factory, before it closed, I mean. He was going to get a big raise and stock and stuff. He had a contract signed by Mr. Sterling and everything. The bank gave him a big loan because of it, and we got a new house and it was really nice, but then the factory closed all of a sudden and he lost his job and he couldn't pay the bank. My dad told Mr. Sterling he had to honor the contract, and Mr. Sterling just laughed at him, and I guess my dad kind of snapped and punched him. It was a stupid thing to do, but after losing his job and the house and everything, I guess he just had enough, you know? Mr. Sterling wasn't really hurt or anything, not bad at least, and he could have dropped the charges, but he wouldn't. My mom even tried pleading with him, but he just laughed at her, too. My dad had to spend some time in jail for assaulting him, and now he has a record. He was going to be a vice president and now he can't even get a job at all anymore. It really sucks."

No wonder Jen didn't have much sympathy for Don Sterling. The guy really had done a number on her family. That wasn't all, though. Mikey needed someone to talk to, and we were ready to listen. Some people think interrogating a suspect is all about being a hard case and grilling the guy, but sometimes to be a good detective you also have to be a good therapist—a lot of times the best way to get information is to just keep your mouth shut and let the patient unload. And unload Mikey did.

"The truth is I wanted to shoot him," he admitted matter-of-factly. I think my jaw dropped open. No wonder Jen didn't want him talking to us. He was about to confess!

"At least I thought I did. I was happy when I pulled the trigger and he fell down like he'd been shot. It felt good. Like sometimes during a football game, I pretend the quarterback is really Mr. Sterling, and when I sack him it feels even better than just a regular sack, because it's kind of like getting a little bit of revenge, even if it's just pretend. Seeing him on the ground at the reenactment was kind of like that. Only it turned out that he wasn't pretending, and it didn't feel so good anymore. It felt worse than anything. Like I'd been the one who killed him."

Mikey ran out of steam and buried his head in his hands, racked with guilt. Joe and I were both literally on the edge of our seats. There was a chance the whole case could be wrapped up right there.

"Were you? The one who killed him?" I blurted.

"I—I don't know," Mike said, shaking his head.

"How can you not know?" Joe almost shouted. The suspense was driving us nuts.

"When the police interviewed me after the reenactment, they said I had a motive because of what happened with my dad and that I could have loaded the gun for real if I wanted," Mikey continued. "They even knew about the target shooting merit patches I got at camp when I was a kid, because Deputy Hixson was my counselor, and they said it would have been an easy shot for me. I told them I didn't do it, because, you know, I didn't. I mean, at least I don't think I did it."

"Um, Mikey, isn't whether you shot Don Sterling something you should be fairly certain about?" I asked what should have seemed like an obvious question.

"Well, yeah, that's what I thought too," Mikey agreed, "but I got to thinking about it last night, and I don't think I did it, but what if, like, I did, but by accident?"

"But how do you accidentally load a musket with live ammunition without realizing it?" I asked. I was trying not to get frustrated, but I couldn't tell if he was trying to confess or if he had just taken one too many hits to the helmet.

"Did you load your musket with an actual musket ball?" Joe prodded.

"I don't think so," Mikey said. "Not on purpose at least."

"You have to know if you loaded a musket ball, Mikey," Joe said, trying to reason with him. "You can't accidentally shoot somebody with an unloaded musket."

"What if there was something wrong with my gun, you know? Or maybe I did it wrong? I paid really close attention at the gun safety class, and I've gone over it in my head, like, a hundred times and I think I did everything right, but what if I didn't?"

"That's really unlikely, Mikey," I told him. "Like just about impossible unlikely. You have to actually load the ball down the barrel after you put in the powder and then ram it down with the ramrod. You would have remembered that."

"But I aimed right at him!" Mikey protested. "I aimed right at his heart, and that's where they said he was shot. And when I pulled the trigger, he fell like I had really shot him. It all felt so real."

Mikey sniffled like he was holding back tears and wiped his nose on a big forearm. I had never heard a suspect try so hard to convince us he was guilty. I still couldn't tell if he was confessing to actually having done something wrong or if this was just a case of misplaced guilt. You'd be surprised how many suspects love to talk, even if it means accidentally incriminating themselves while trying to deny a crime. Mikey, on the other hand, looked miserable, and it sounded like he actually did want to incriminate himself, he just wasn't doing a very good job of it.

"There were a lot of people firing muskets all at the same time, Mikey," I reassured him. I was actually feeling bad for the big guy. "I'm pretty sure you weren't the only one aiming at the Don. Mr. Lakin as much as told everyone to. It couldn't have been you unless your musket was loaded."

"But what if I loaded it subcontinentally, you know, and didn't even realize it?"

Joe looked baffled as he tried to figure out what Mikey had just said. I jumped in and did my best to translate.

"You mean what if you did it subconsciously?" I asked. It was a good thing Mikey was good at football, because I don't think he was going to be winning any academic scholarships anytime soon.

"Yeah, that!" Mikey said. "I know it sounds crazy, but what if because I hated him so much I subconsciously blacked out for a minute and put a real bullet in the gun? I don't remember anything like that, but then I wouldn't, right? Like this one time I sleepwalked, and Jen found me in the kitchen all covered in crumbs because I'd eaten, like, everything in the pantry, even the uncooked spaghetti and sardines, and I hate sardines, and then when I woke up I didn't remember doing it at all. What if it was like that, but just a lot worse?"

Mikey was right—his theory sounded crazy. Crazy enough that the police would probably slap cuffs on him if they heard it.

Defense lawyers sometimes try to claim their clients blacked out and had temporary amnesia when they committed a crime so they can plea temporary insanity. Usually, though, it's just a desperate last-ditch attempt to justify the actions of a guilty criminal who doesn't have a legitimate defense. It almost never works. If Mikey went to the police with his theory, they'd peg him as a guilt-ridden killer trying to clear his conscience without actually confessing to what he'd done. And they might be right. But even if it was just a case of overactive imagination, it would still shoot him straight to the top of Chief Olaf's suspect list.

"Jen told me not to say anything to anyone. She didn't even want to know." Mikey sounded ashamed. "Like maybe she thought I really could have done it or something. She told me to keep it to myself or people would think I did it and I'd lose my shot at a scholarship and maybe end up in jail and broke like Dad. I don't want to let Jen and my folks down, but I can't stop thinking about it. I mean, even if I didn't do it, I still feel like it's my fault for wanting him dead that way. And what if I really did shoot him? Not knowing, it's eating me up. Mr. Sterling wasn't a good person, but he didn't deserve to die. I don't know if I could live with myself if I really killed someone, even if it was the Don."

Mikey's phone buzzed, and he looked down at the screen with a defeated expression.

"That's Jen," he sighed. "I have to go. If you guys find out anything that—well, you know, even if it's bad, I want to know. And please don't tell Jen I talked to you guys, okay? Thanks."

Mikey lumbered off, hanging his head like he'd just missed the tackle that lost his team the championship. I didn't think the part about us not telling Jen would be a problem, at least. I didn't think she had any intention of talking to us. As for the rest of it, well, from the baffled look on Joe's face, I could tell we both felt about the same way. The Griffin siblings had done a good job of turning our morning inside out and then upside down.

We were going to have a lot to discuss, but we were going to have to discuss it later. There was someone else at the top of our list we had to talk to first. The stepson of Mikey's maybe-victim had just walked around the corner.

PRECIOUS METALS

12

JOE

I DIDN'T KNOW WHAT TO MAKE OF MIKEY'S STRANGE sorta-kinda-not-really-maybe confession. If there was anything to his half-baked theories about the Don's murder, it was going to complicate things even more. Like this case wasn't tough enough already!

At least the idea that Jen might have flipped out on us because she was just trying to protect her brother made me feel a little better about the scene in the cafeteria (looking after a brother was one thing us Hardy boys could definitely relate to). I just wasn't so sure she would feel the same way about me in reverse, though, especially after she warned us away from Mikey and we went ahead and talked to him anyway. I didn't think it would matter to her that he came to us. Thoughts about Jen and Mikey Griffin would have to wait for now, though.

Don Sterling's stepson Calvin was heading up the outside steps to the second-floor hallway.

Calvin was our only inside source into the Don's personal life, and talking to him was a top priority. I'd had a few classes with him, and he wasn't a bad guy. The "Silver Son" got a lot of grief from the other kids because of who his stepdad was, but it wasn't his fault his mom had married Bayport's version of Scrooge McDuck.

I was surprised he was even at school after what had happened to his stepdad the day before. And from his reaction when he saw us running up to him, he didn't seem that broken up about it.

"Hey, guys, what's up?" he asked nonchalantly.

"We're really sorry about your stepdad, Calvin," Frank said, and I nodded solemnly.

"Oh, yeah, thanks. Sucks, huh? I mean, I wasn't all that close to Don, but my mom is pretty upset about it. I heard you guys were trying to find out who did it."

So much for keeping a low profile.

"If it's cool, we were hoping you could tell us anything you think might help us figure out why someone would want to harm your stepdad," I said. "It could really make a big difference."

"Sure. I don't know how much I can help, but I'm happy to do whatever I can. It would make my mom feel a lot better if you can catch the killer," Calvin said. "Oh, and the police already talked to me and my mom. Before you get any ideas she might have had something to do with it, she doesn't need Don's money. Not that there's going to be much left to inherit anyway."

Frank and I did a Hardy double take on that one. Everybody knew Don Sterling was one of the wealthiest people in town. Calvin saw our surprise.

"If someone killed him for the money, then they're in for a real shock. His high-roller thing was mostly just an act," Calvin said.

"That can't be right. He was the museum's biggest bene-factor," Frank said in disbelief.

"Nah, that's just what Don wanted everyone to think. Most of it was my mom's money—she just let Don take credit for it. A lot of it came from the city, too. And he only donated the ship to the historical society in the first place because he was going to lose the property he found it on and figured it would be good for his image after the whole factory fiasco. He about threw a fit when Mr. Lakin found all those crates full of expensive artifacts. He was even going to get his lawyers to try to take everything back. I overheard him telling my mom about it. I guess he decided not to, but if he'd known anything on that ship would end up being worth so much, he never would have let it out of his sight to begin with."

"I guess that explains all the arguing with Mr. Lakin over what he could sell at auction," Frank said.

"Ha!" Calvin laughed. "Don was always arguing with

everyone over money lately. He was in way over his head with bad investments and ended up having to sell his stake in the factory for, like, pennies on the dollar just to pay off some of Sterling Industries' debts. My mom's pretty much been supporting him for a while now."

POP. That was the sound of Calvin bursting the bubble on what pretty much everybody thought they knew about Don Sterling. A lot of people in Bayport might take satisfaction in learning that the Don's business was going belly-up, but for Frank and me, Don Sterling being broke just raised a whole new slew of questions we didn't have answers to. To figure out who else might have benefited from the Don's death, we were going to have to find out more about his other business dealings. I was about to hit Calvin with some follow-up questions when Frank jumped in.

"Where did you get that?" he asked, pointing to the gold key chain in Calvin's hand.

On closer inspection, I could tell why Frank was so interested in it. The large gold coin dangling from the key ring looked a lot like the one in the museum display about the lost British treasure.

"What, this?" Calvin held up the key chain. "I made it in shop. Pretty sweet, huh?"

"Supersweet," Frank said. "Where did you get the coin?"

"Found it in the coin tray at home. It must have gotten mixed in with Don's or my mom's change, like when you get one of those Canadian quarters by accident. I didn't think they'd miss it, so I took it to shop to use the drill press and put a nice key ring on it." Calvin beamed over his new accessory.

"Do you mind if I see it?" Frank asked, and Calvin handed over the key chain.

I leaned over Frank's shoulder as he examined it. The coin was rough edged and not quite perfectly round. It had a picture of an old-timey British lady on one side and a crowned lion and a unicorn on the other side.

"Is it okay if I take a picture?" Frank asked.

"Sure." Calvin shrugged. Frank snapped a couple of quick pics and handed back the key chain.

"I've got to get to class, but if there's anything else I can do to help, just let me know." Calvin walked off down the hall, the gold coin dangling from his hand.

I knew the look on Frank's face. It was that nerd-fueled rush of excitement he gets when we make an especially geeky breakthrough on a case.

"You don't think that's just some random coin that got mixed in with the Don's change, do you?" I asked.

"It might have accidentally gotten mixed up with the Don's change, but I don't think it was random," Frank answered.

"You think it's strange the Don had a copy of the replica coin from the exhibit at the museum about the lost British treasure?" I asked, trying to figure out why it had Frank so amped up.

"I don't think that was a replica," he said. "The coin in the display is cheap gold-plated tin; I held it before they put it behind glass. Calvin's coin was twice as heavy and looked gold all the way through where he drilled the hole. He might not realize it, but I'm pretty sure the coin dangling from his key chain is pure gold."

"No way," I said, starting to share some of Frank's excitement. "How would the Don have gotten ahold of a real coin from the treasure?"

"I don't know, but I think that coin is the real deal, Joe," Frank said reverently.

"How do we find out for sure?" I asked.

We both thought about it for a second. The answer came to us at the same time. "Murph!"

Murph "the Collector" Murphy was probably the only dude at Bayport High who knew more obscure facts about random stuff than Frank did. Murph got the nickname "the Collector" because that's what he does—collect stuff. All kinds of stuff. If it can be collected, there's a good chance he either collects it or knows all about it. Stamps, vintage Japanese toy robots, baseball cards, comic books, butterflies, apothecary jars (yeah, I don't know what they are either), and, of course, coins. Murph was our man.

I sometimes joke with Frank about being a nerd. Well, Murph took nerdism to another level. He turned it into a fashion statement. When we caught up to him outside the library, he was sporting a perfectly tied bow tie, an argyle sweater-vest, and thick old-school black-framed glasses. But this wasn't your typical frumpy classic nerd look. It was all perfectly coordinated, expensive *GQ* fashion kind of stuff. The look was geek chic hipster, and Murph had the nerd-tastic confidence to pull it off, too. He didn't care if people thought he was different, and you had to admire him for it.

Frank showed Murph the pictures. If he had been a car-toon character, his eyes would have turned into big gold coins and popped right out of their sockets, that's how wide they got when he saw Calvin's key chain.

"Is that what I think it is?" he asked in awe.

"We were hoping you could tell us," Frank said.

"If it's real, it's one of the Queen Charlotte gold pieces from the King's Pride Treasure," Murph affirmed, and Frank glowed.

"They're like the Holy Grail for a lot of coin collectors," Murph said, launching into a lecture, with Frank and me as his eager pupils. "One or two have popped up at auction in England, but they're, like, super rare. No one has ever found one in America before, not that anyone knows about any-way, and people have been hunting for them for, like, two hundred and fifty years. King George had them minted in a single run in 1775 for the sole purpose of helping fund the war in America, but they vanished before ever making it into circulation in the colonies. There are rumors that the British ship carrying them was intercepted by the Continental Navy off the coast not far from Bayport, but no one knows for sure because none of the coins ever turned up. The shipment was called the King's Pride because they're the only gold currency Old George ever let the Royal Mint press with Queen Charlotte's image while she was alive. And they'd be worth a king's fortune to whoever found them now."

Murph flipped between the pictures of the front and back of the coin.

"This sure looks real enough from the pictures. The detail on the unicorn is unique to Queen Charlotte's family seal. I'd have to see it for myself to know for certain if this one is just a good fake or not. If it's real?" Murph whistled. "It's worth a whole lot more than its weight in gold, I can tell you that. Usually coin valuation depends on condition— and I'd like to give a piece of my mind to whoever went and desecrated it with a drill, by the way—but even with that big old hole in it, that puppy all by itself could be worth more than a lot of people make in a year."

If Murph was right, we'd stumbled on a second mystery. Frank looked like he'd won the lottery. This wasn't just a murder investigation anymore. It had turned into a treasure hunt.

THE FUGITIVE 13

FRANK

URPH WANDERED OFF, MUTTERING to himself in a daze, like he'd just seen the Loch Ness Monster strolling the halls of Bayport High. I could relate. That excited-kid-like feeling I got while looking at the fake coin in the museum display? Multiply that times a million. If the coin on Calvin's key chain was what Murph and I thought it was, then the Hardy boys were about to add a new specialty to our investigative repertoire: treasure hunters.

I didn't want to get too far ahead of myself—the coin could still be a fake—but right now, there was a good chance Calvin was walking around with a small fortune's worth of the King's Pride Treasure in his pocket, thinking it was just a cool trinket that got mixed up with his stepdad's change.

And if he was, that meant Mr. Sterling may have stumbled on some serious gold before he checked out.

"If the Don discovered even a small part of the treasure, it could have solved a lot of his money troubles," Joe observed.

"At least it would have if he hadn't been killed first," I pointed out.

"Do you think he realized the significance of what he had?" Joe asked.

"If it got thrown in with his change, then either he didn't know what it was or he'd found enough of the coins that he could afford to be careless with this one," I said, thrilled by the idea that the coin might be the tip of a golden iceberg.

"Maybe more importantly, did anyone else realize the significance of what he found?" Joe asked, and my detective senses started tingling. I could feel the beginnings of a theory brewing.

Our conversation with Calvin had revealed a pair of shockers: The Don may have been in possession of a gold coin belonging to a legendary long-lost treasure, and Bayport's biggest tycoon was just about broke. There was another person involved in the case also having money troubles, and it coincidentally (or maybe not) happened to be the Don's sworn enemy. It was almost time for my history class, and I'd just added another line of inquiry for Mr. Lakin.

Joe and I agreed to reconvene after school when I'd gotten done talking to Mr. Lakin. My apprehension about having to question Mr. Lakin as a suspect and pry into his personal life was offset by the case's new golden twist. Our teacher's possible involvement was still gnawing at me, though. Joe could tell I was worried.

"Good luck, bro." Joe encouraged me with a slap on the back. "I think we're on the verge of something big."

Bolstered by my brother's confidence, I headed for Mr. Lakin's classroom. I walked in the door just before the bell and was greeted with yet another surprise—a classroom full of kids but no teacher. Mr. Lakin was known for his punctuality. He was always on time, and he demanded the same of his students. He locked the door the second the bell rang, and if you were a half second late, well, then you were out of luck. This time, though, the bell rang and the classroom door remained open. Mr. Lakin was a no-show.

A minute later Mr. Carr came in and told us the class was canceled. He wouldn't say why. Everybody started buzzing and speculating that it had something to do with the Don's murder. I chased after Mr. Carr to find out more, but he told me he wasn't at liberty to say. I thought about taking the opportunity to ask Mr. Carr some questions about his involvement in the reenactment, since his name had made our suspect list as well, but I figured tracking down Mr. Lakin was the higher priority.

I got my answer about Mr. Lakin's absence a minute later when I accidentally ran into Chief Olaf coming out of the principal's office. I tried heading in the opposite direction to avoid him, but . . .

"Hardy!" the Chief yelled.

I wasn't quick enough.

"Yes, sir." I turned to face him with the same guilty look I usually get around the chief even when I haven't done anything wrong. It was habit, I guess.

"Don't worry, Frank, you're not in trouble," he reassured me . . . sort of. "Yet."

"Is this about Mr. Lakin not showing up for class?" I asked, hoping to take advantage of the chief's good (i.e., not awful) mood to gain some information.

"Unfortunately, yes," he replied uneasily. "I know he's something of a mentor to you, and I was hoping he might have said something to you that will help us find him."

"He's missing?" I asked in alarm.

"I'm afraid he is." The chief looked disturbed. "He stood me up at the station for a follow-up interview during the break in his schedule at one and then didn't turn up for his classes. We have to assume he's fled."

"You have evidence that he did it?" I asked, my stomach dropping.

"You know I can't comment on that, Frank. But innocent people don't usually go on the run from the police. It doesn't look good. I'm sorry." Chief Olaf put a hand on my shoulder. "If you do hear from him, I want you to tell him to come in, and then you call me immediately. I've known Rollie for a long time, but if this thing turns into a manhunt, I won't be able to help him."

The chief sighed deeply and walked off looking anguished. This case was taking a real toll on him. I knew how he felt. I also knew how much the museum meant to Mr. Lakin. If he'd taken off, then the situation must really be desperate. Especially with a sick wife in the hospital. Chief Olaf was right. It didn't look good.

I started back down the hall to find Joe and break the news. I was about to pass Mr. Lakin's classroom when I stopped. The door had been left open a crack. I looked back over my shoulder. Chief Olaf was gone, and there weren't any teachers in sight. The opportunity was too inviting to ignore.

I slid in the door and did a quick survey of Mr. Lakin's desk. I didn't expect to find much. Mr. Lakin's pretty neat. The drawers were locked, no surprise there, and there wasn't a lot on the desk itself, but sometimes a little can be plenty. A small white card poked out from between the pages of a compact notepad full of Mr. Lakin's indecipherable chicken-scratch scribbles.

I flipped the pad open to find a familiar business card with the name DIRK BISHOP and the words ANTIQUES & ANTIQUITIES embossed in gold. Mr. Lakin had scrawled four barely legible words on the piece of paper beneath the card. It took me a few seconds to decipher what it said: "Bay Breeze Inn—Noon."

I studied the page. It looked like Mr. Lakin had planned to meet Bishop this afternoon just an hour before he failed to show up at the police station. If he'd made it to the meeting at the Bay Breeze, then Dirk Bishop may have been the last person to see him before he disappeared.

What did Bishop want to see Mr. Lakin about? And what could have happened at that meeting to compel Mr. Lakin to vanish?

I stared at Bishop's business card, hoping it would provide the answer. Something about the card was bothering me, but I couldn't quite put my finger on it. Sunlight from the window glinted off the embossed letters in a flash of gold.

I smiled. We were going to have a talk with our snooty English visitor.

THE SECOND MAN

14

JOE

I WAS SITTING ON THE WALL IN FRONT OF THE school, still trying to make sense of all our new information, when Frank burst through the door yelling.

"Mr. Lakin's gone! The police think he fled. I don't know where he went, but I think I know who might."

Before I knew it, Frank had made the dash all the way across the courtyard to the wall and was dragging me along after him, still talking.

"We've got to get to the Bay Breeze Inn. I'll explain on the way."

Frank wasn't wasting any time, and for good reason.

"The business card you found on Mr. Lakin's desk makes Bishop a direct link between the victim and the prime suspect," I agreed with Frank after he brought me up to speed.

Yup, the rude British antiques dealer we'd had the displeasure of meeting after the reenactment had just turned into a major player in our mystery. He had come to America to meet with Don Sterling, but Sterling was killed during the reenactment around the same time Bishop arrived, and the man we'd told him to talk to instead was Mr. Lakin. Judging from Frank's discovery, Bishop had taken our advice.

"If their meeting took place, it was one degree of separation from Mr. Lakin's vanishing act," Frank said.

"Which means Bishop might know what happened to him," I added.

"Whatever went down at that meeting may hold the key to the whole mystery," Frank confirmed.

Frank had uncovered our biggest lead, and we followed it to the Bay Breeze Inn, a quaint little hotel a short walk from the harbor where the *Resolve* was docked. Sophie Drew, a Bayport High kid who'd graduated the year before, was working the front desk. She recognized us from school and greeted us with a big smile.

"Sure, the snobby English guy," Sophie said perkily when I asked if Mr. Bishop was staying there. "He checked in last night. I haven't seen him around today, though."

She tried ringing his room for us. No answer. We thanked her and stepped outside to try the international phone number on Bishop's business card. The voice that picked up had Bishop's distinctive proper British accent, but it was only a recording. The message said he would be back in London on Tuesday night.

"Tuesday night! He isn't planning on staying long if he's supposed to be back in England tomorrow," I said with concern.

Frank did some quick math. "London is five hours ahead of us, and it's a seven-hour flight. If he plans to be back in London tomorrow night, that means he's got to be flying out tomorrow morning."

"That doesn't give us much time to find him before he wraps up whatever business he had with Don Sterling and Mr. Lakin and hightails it out of town," I said, my concern growing.

"Whatever that business was, it must have been important enough for him to fly all the way across the Atlantic Ocean and then turn around and fly all the way back two days later," Frank observed.

"Not much of a vacation, is it?" I asked, not that either of us really thought he was here on vacation. The question was, why was he here and how did it fit with Don Sterling's murder and Mr. Lakin's disappearance?

"So why would an antiques dealer go to all that trouble? None of the antiques on display in the museum are for sale," Frank quizzed me.

"You think the Don was trying to sell artifacts from the *Resolve* behind the museum's back? We know from Calvin that he needed cash," I said, picking up his line of thought.

"If Sterling was selling something, Bishop must have thought it was pretty darn valuable for him to go to all the trouble and expense of coming here," Frank said, running his fingers over the fancy embossed gold lettering on Bishop's business card. "I've got a feeling I might know what he's after. I think it's time we find out more about our mysterious guest."

There was a computer for guests in the lobby of the Bay Breeze Inn, and Sophie gave us the okay to use it. We sat down and typed in a search for "Dirk Bishop, Antiques and Antiquities, London." There was nothing unusual at first, but a little bit of online detective work revealed that Dirk Bishop was more than just your typical antiques dealer. He specialized in a very specific kind of antique—sunken British treasure.

His name popped up in a London *Times* article about the attempted recovery of an eighteenth-century treasure from a British East India Company cargo ship that had been carrying more than a ton of gold and silver ingots when it sank near the British Isles. The article said the salvage team claimed to have come up empty, but just a few weeks later Bishop and one of the treasure divers were suspected of illegally dealing similar gold ingots on the international black market. He had also been investigated a lot closer to home on our side of the pond for violating the US Abandoned Shipwreck Act by salvaging artifacts from another sunken British cargo vessel off the coast of Rhode Island.

"So why would a treasure hunter from London travel all the way to America for a meeting with Don Sterling in tiny little Bayport?" Frank asked with a gleam in his eye.

"When we told Bishop that the Don was dead, he wanted to know who else he could talk to about items recovered when the *Resolve* was restored," I recalled. "And he sounded all weasel-like when he said it too!"

"I don't think he wanted to talk about muskets and sabers," Frank hinted.

"But he would have been very interested in the gold coin Calvin found in Don Sterling's coin tray," I said. Frank nodded.

"He would if it was real. Calvin said Sterling decided not to sue the historical society to get back the stuff they found on the *Resolve*, but it doesn't make any sense that a broke guy with the Don's reputation would just give up on a fortune in valuable artifacts."

"Not unless he had a line on an even bigger fortune in valuable artifacts the museum hadn't found," I said, giving Frank the answer he wanted to hear. I liked the ring of it.

"Okay, let's say the Don did find a treasure that could be worth maybe even millions of dollars. Maybe somebody else found it too," Frank theorized.

"Then Calvin might be wrong about someone killing his stepdad for the money, after all," I jumped in to finish the thought.

We chewed on that for a minute before I reluctantly

brought the theory full circle. "Don Sterling wasn't the only one involved in the museum who desperately needed money."

"Mrs. Lakin's hospital bills," Frank said, sounding deflated.

It didn't feel great to be right about the documents we'd found in Mr. Lakin's old office aboard the *Resolve* maybe being important, but the debt gave him real incentive to get his hands on some quick cash by whatever means necessary.

"Both Don Sterling and Mr. Lakin needed money, right? And if Bishop really is in Bayport on a treasure hunt, the Don may have found a boatload of it before someone killed him. . . ."

"Or a shipload," Frank corrected, but the interruption lacked his usual enthusiasm.

We were both on the same disturbing train of thought, and it wasn't a smooth ride: If the Don had found a shipload of treasure before he was murdered and a day later the prime murder suspect met with a black market treasure dealer, then skipped out on the police, well, it starts to make the prime suspect look pretty suspicious. We knew Mr. Lakin had the means (his experience firing a gun on horseback in the mounted police) and the opportunity (firing a pistol at the Don during the reenactment), and now, because of his money troubles, the gold would give him a solid motive as well. It made his disappearance right after meeting with Bishop seem even less like the action of an innocent man. Even worse, if Mr. Lakin had fled, it probably meant that whatever business he had with Bishop was already finished. And if they had taken the money and run, then we might never find the killer or the treasure in Bayport.

I felt a charge of excitement along with my sadness at how Mr. Lakin's role in the mystery was shaping up. The existence of Bayport's legendary lost treasure suddenly seemed like more than just a fun little-kid fantasy, and the possibility that Don Sterling's murder may have had something to do with it was turning into a plausible theory.

"The Gold theory," Frank said aloud.

So now we had a theory. What we didn't have was a way to investigate it further. Not until Mr. Lakin or Dirk Bishop turned up. Until then we were stalled.

Frank asked Sophie to call us as soon as Mr. Bishop came in, explaining that the museum staff wanted to surprise him with a thank-you gift for coming all the way from London. When you think about it, Frank's story stretched the truth only a little—my brother technically was part of the museum staff after all, and we really did want to surprise Bishop. If he was involved in the Don's murder and he knew we were onto him, he wouldn't wait around to greet us.

Time was running out, and so were our leads. Stumped, we decided to employ one of our most scientific investigative problem-solving strategies: one of Aunt Trudy's home-cooked meals.

Detectives have to eat too, and I've found that a full belly can do wonders for mental clarity. We'd made breakthroughs on more than one mystery while hashing things out across the kitchen table and chowing down on our aunt's cooking.

When we arrived home, there were Revolutionary War–themed plates of fish and chips waiting for us. Aunt Trudy had even wrapped them in newspaper like they do in England. She'd used delicate fillets of locally caught red snapper, lightly coated in a perfectly seasoned batter of her own concoction paired with a chip trio made from patriotically colored red, white, and blue potatoes.

It tasted as good as it looked. I didn't have much of an appetite, though. It had been an eventful day, and my brain was working overtime trying to sort it all out. We'd come up with our first theory to work with, but as Frank likes to remind me, in science an unproven theory is merely a hypothesis, and we still had a lot of other information to process as well if we were going to crack this case.

My thoughts wandered back to Jen and her blowup in the cafeteria. With everything else that had happened today, I'd been so focused on how it fit the investigation I hadn't really had a chance to think about how it made me feel. Now I did, and it stung. Especially how she'd told me to stay away from her. I had really liked Jen. It dawned on me that I didn't really know her that well. I could totally relate to her wanting to protect her brother, but how she'd gone about it showed a dark side. It's something I would have to come to grips with if I did manage to get back on her good side.

Not that that was likely to happen anytime soon. Not if she found out Mikey had gone behind her back to talk to us. His mixed-up kind-of confession had been bugging me all day.

I try not to judge people, and I don't just mean during an investigation, but in real life, too. Our dad always says that the best way not to misjudge someone is to not judge them in the first place. But before today I'd pretty much written Mikey off as a dumb, obnoxious jock without even giving him a chance. Okay, so maybe the dumb jock part wasn't so far off, but after listening to him pour his heart out to us outside the cafeteria, there turned out to be a lot more to the big, sensitive lug than I ever would have given him credit for. You kind of had to feel for the guy.

It was an odd thought to have about a murder suspect, and I had to be careful not to lose my objectivity—there's more than one way to misjudge someone, and Mikey could still be our killer. The murder had really shaken him up, though. He could have kept being angry at Don Sterling even though he was dead, like Jen had, but he hadn't. He sounded truly sorry the Don had been hurt, even though he had every reason to hate the guy for what he'd done to his family.

Mikey didn't just sound sorry, though. He also sounded guilty. There's a big difference between feeling guilty and actually being guilty, though, and I think that's what was bothering me so much. In Mikey's case, I didn't know which was which. His story didn't add up, not the way he told it.

What I did know was that he really seemed to believe he had shot the Don.

So had Mikey gotten revenge on the guy who put his father in jail? And was he just playing dumb to clear his conscience and/or misdirect our investigation? That's what the police would probably assume. I didn't think Mikey was smart enough to pull off such a complex crime. But continuing to underestimate a suspect is a good way to get fooled. I'd already had everything I thought I knew about both Griffin kids turned upside down once that day, and if you keep repeating the same mistake, you kind of deserve to get fooled.

So maybe he had done it. Or maybe he was having some kind of posttraumatic stress thing from witnessing a murder. As real as the reenactment had seemed to me, it would have taken on a whole other level of reality for Mikey. In his mind, he'd aimed at the Don and fired his musket, and the Don had ended up dead, so it must have been his fault. Even if you were shooting blanks, firing a real gun at a man who ends up shot dead at the same time had to mess with your head big-time. It would kind of be like willing someone dead. There were probably a lot of Colonial reenactors who had fired their muskets at the Don—Mr. Lakin had encouraged them to—and I wondered if there were other people struggling with guilt because of it too. I mean, what if it had been me? I fired a musket during the reenactment too. I had gotten lucky; nobody on the other end of my sights had ended up with a hole in their chest. They could have, though. It was chilling to think about.

"Do you think there's anything to what Mikey told us?" I asked Frank.

"Hmm?" Frank looked up. He'd been staring at his plate, lost in his own thoughts too.

"Do you think Mikey really could have somehow shot the Don without knowing what he was doing?" I asked again. He thought about it for a minute.

"Pretty unlikely," he said through a mouthful of red snapper. "I mean, a musket ball didn't accidentally fall down his barrel, and real episodes of temporary amnesia are about as rare as gold coins. And even if he did black out for a moment during the reenactment, he still would've had to bring a musket ball with him, right? It's hard to imagine someone doing that without it being premeditated. I guess he could be lying to us, but it would be hard to prove without more evidence or an actual confession. We'll talk to him tomorrow and see if his story changes."

We were at another dead end. I stabbed at Aunt Trudy's Revolutionary War–themed red, white, and blue fries with my fork and thought about Aunt Trudy under her red, white, and blue sun umbrella at the reenactment. Ha! Actually, it was a double "Ha!" I laughed at the image of Aunt Trudy and then had an "aha!" moment—she'd been shooting video of the reenactment! I'd had a hunch Aunt Trudy's meal would lead to some sort of revelation.

In all the excitement of the past day, we'd forgotten all about it. It wasn't likely to break the mystery open or anything—whatever Aunt Trudy caught in the video would have happened in plain sight of a few hundred people, and the police probably already knew about it—but it was still worth watching to see if it shook anything loose. I ran the idea past Frank.

"Beats sitting around and feeling useless!" Frank agreed cheerily.

"True. And maybe it'll at least help us rule out Mikey's crazy theories."

We got the video from Aunt Trudy and watched it full screen on the computer. The angle was pretty wide, so we got an overview of the field without a lot of close-up detail. Even when she zoomed in, the image still captured a big chunk of the action, but there was also a lot you couldn't see, and the people we wanted to watch weren't always in the frame. We tried to focus on Mr. Lakin and Mikey along with Amir, Mr. Carr, Pete Carson, Rob Hernandez, and the other suspects on our list. I took notes as we watched, breaking down the reenactment into moments of action we could refer back to.

Mr. Lakin looked on proudly in his general's uniform, his saber and pistol swinging from his belt as Bernie handed out muskets to the Colonial militia. Mr. Carr gave a dramatic salute to Mr. Lakin when he got his weapon. Mikey was the next suspect to get his musket. Mr. Carr went over to say something to Mikey after he got his gun, but there was no way to tell what. It looked like they were going over some detail of how to load the musket. Then the camera panned away from Bernie and Mr. Lakin handing out the muskets and went over to the British side.

A few minutes later, Mikey and Amir were back in the picture, palling around before the battle. Mikey was laughing and gesturing wildly with both hands as he told a joke or something. As the reenactment got ready to start, the infantrymen formed a drill line, and Mr. Lakin made a show of doing inspections. He straightened Amir's lapel and took Mikey's musket to examine it before handing it back and moving on to the next soldier.

Then the chaos started. The first cannon went off, and the whole field got real smoky real fast from all the shooting. With so much going on, it was hard to follow all the action. Knowing what happened next, I almost turned away when Mr. Lakin charged forward on his horse and Don Sterling collapsed. There were so many guns going off at the same time, there was no way to tell from watching the video who'd fired the real shot, and it was too hazy and far away to see if Mikey had done anything unusual when he loaded his musket. The shot could have come from Mr. Lakin's gun or Mikey's. It also could have come from Amir's, Mr. Carr's, Pete's, or a lot of the other militiamen as well.

Frank had that pale look about him again, and I knew he had the same queasy feeling I did. What we'd just watched wasn't for show. A man had really been shot.

So far, watching the video hadn't answered any questions. All it had done for the investigation was make the investigators feel ill.

"I'm going to catch a quick nap and then we can reconvene to come up with a strategy for the evening." Frank took a deep breath, collapsed on the couch, and started snoring pretty much instantly. As beat as I was, I was way too amped to sleep. I pressed play one more time instead.

A couple of minutes later, I paused and hit rewind. Mikey stood on the baseball field, palling around with Amir before the reenactment, gesturing with both hands open. It wasn't what I saw that caught my eye, it was what I couldn't see.

Mikey's gun.

Amir was still holding a musket, but Mikey wasn't. He must have put it down somewhere off screen, because the gun wasn't anywhere in sight. That's when it hit me. Maybe Mikey had been right.

SWEET DREAMS

15

FRANK

WAS WEARING MY REENACTMENT COSTUME IN my dream, but that wasn't the cool part. The cool part was the cutlass clamped between my teeth and the rope in my hands as I swung across the bow of the *Resolve* to rescue Daphne from Mr. Lakin, who was dressed like a plaid-clad pirate captain. The Plaid Pirate Lakin propped his peg leg on top of a treasure chest and threatened Daphne with a metal-hooked hand. Daphne yelled out my name, and that's when the dream really got weird. Daphne sounded exactly like Joe!

"Frank!" she yelled in Joe's voice. "Wake up, dude!"

When I opened my eyes, the twist in my dream suddenly made a lot more sense. Joe really was yelling my name. Bummer.

"Can it wait, dude? I was having a really awesome dream," I muttered, still half-asleep.

"What if Mikey shooting the Don was premeditated," Joe asked excitedly, "just not by Mikey?"

That opened my eyes all the way. My Daphne-in-distress fantasy was going to have to stay a cliffhanger.

"What have you got?" I asked him.

"It's really been bugging me how sure Mikey seemed about somehow being the one who shot the Don. I mean, he sounded so sincere, but it didn't make any sense. How can you shoot somebody and just not remember it?"

"It would be a neat trick," I agreed.

"Even neater if Mikey wasn't the magician," Joe said. "I think there is a way Mikey could have been onto something with his crazy ideas about his musket being loaded, just not the way he thought."

"I'm listening," I said, now all the way awake.

"I went back and watched the video again, and there are a few times when Mikey's gun is either out of his sight or someone else has it. If Mikey wasn't the only one who had access to his musket before he fired it during the reenactment . . ."

"You think someone could have tampered with it?" I asked reluctantly. Joe was opening up a disturbing new door.

"I think it's possible, at least. There's nothing obvious in the video, but the opportunity would have been there. Everyone just assumed the shooter was working alone, but what if there was a second person involved? The shooter could have had an accomplice, or he could even have been set up."

Setting someone up would be a huge gamble. It was almost too risky and callous to consider.

"What if they missed and hit the wrong person, or the killer miscalculated and the shooter decided to aim at someone else instead?" I said, hoping Joe was wrong. "Talk about cold-blooded."

"We already know the killer has to be one cold, bold hombre to try to assassinate someone in public like that in the first place," Joe pointed out.

"The Second Man theory," I said, giving Joe's theory a name. We've found that classifying our theories sometimes helps us wrap our minds around a mystery and organize our thoughts, especially on a complex case like this one.

"If someone really was that devious and wanted to pick a shooter to take out Don Sterling for them, then Mikey Griffin would be a good bet," I affirmed.

Joe nodded. "He said he was a good shot, and with his family's history with the Don, it wouldn't be hard to guess who Mikey was aiming at."

"Mikey's not the only one," I said. "A lot of people probably aimed at the Don. Mr. Lakin basically told them to."

Not that people needed any encouragement. Even if they thought they were only shooting blanks, it would be hard to resist pretending to take a shot at the guy who'd messed up your life.

Our job had just gotten a lot harder. It was tough enough already just trying to figure out which gun had fired the shot; now, even if we did, it might not be the real bad guy's. We didn't just have to look at who had motive, we also had to look at who had access to the guns of the people with motive. Joe was right about Mikey, though: If there was a fall guy, he was a good candidate.

Joe had flagged the spots in the video where Mikey put down his gun or when someone else had it. He skipped ahead from Mikey receiving his musket to Mr. Carr helping Mikey with his gun to musketless Mikey goofing around with Amir. Joe was right: Someone totally would have had the opportunity to tamper with Mikey's gun. Both Mr. Carr and Amir knew Mikey well enough to have his confidence, and both of them had the opportunity.

It was common knowledge that Mr. Carr hated the Don, and he had the acting skills to pull off a deception. He also had a flair for the dramatic and a love of old English plays with intricate revenge plots and leading men with guilty consciences. The pieces fit, but could our own drama teacher really have used one of his students to exact his revenge for him? He would have had the chance.

So would Amir, Mikey's buddy from their time together in detention. When Aunt Trudy moved the camera away from Amir and Mikey goofing around, you could still see Mikey in the background, but Amir had stepped out of frame. When he reappeared, he was carrying Mikey's musket along with his own.

I liked Amir. We used to study together before Don

Sterling shut down the factory. After his parents lost their jobs, everything changed, though, and he stopped caring about class. You knew things must have gotten pretty bad at home, because he'd gone from one of Bayport High's brightest students to one of its biggest troublemakers in no time flat. It was like he was a different guy. But murder? I didn't like the idea of an old friend turning into a devious killer.

Not that I liked the next possible Second Man suspect any better. Joe fast-forwarded to Mikey having his musket inspected in the drill line. By Mr. Lakin. The angle was on Mr. Lakin's back, so we couldn't see exactly what he was doing, but he held the gun long enough to leave the possibility open. Thinking about our history teacher using a student to pull the trigger for him was even more disturbing than suspecting him of pulling the trigger himself.

I took some comfort in the fact that Joe's Second Man theory was still purely hypothetical. The second person could have been someone we suspected or someone we hadn't thought of yet, or the killer could have acted alone and there might not be any "Second Man" at all. We didn't have any proof, and for all we knew it was just another wild-goose chase.

Even so, just the idea of it was enough to turn my stomach. And until we had some proof one way or another, we couldn't eliminate the possibility that it was a valid hypothesis.

"There could be a lot more to this case than we figured," Joe said.

"You mean one mystery shooter using a fake Revolutionary War battle as cover to secretly load a 250-year-old firearm with real ammunition and publicly assassinate Bayport's most notorious businessman with the whole town watching isn't enough?" I shot back. I should have known better than to even ask. There's always more.

But for now, we'd reached another standstill. We now had two theories to explore—my Gold theory and Joe's Second Man theory. We just didn't have any way to explore them, not from our den. Our forty-eight-hour clock was ticking, and the trails on Mr. Lakin and Dirk Bishop were growing colder by the second. By tomorrow afternoon it would be two full days since the Don's murder, and the statistical chances of ever catching his killer would plummet. We had an even shorter window to find Bishop. By tomorrow morning he'd be sitting pretty somewhere over the Atlantic, and whatever role he'd played in this mystery would probably stay a mystery.

I was contemplating hitting the streets of Bayport and wandering until we stumbled onto a new lead when my phone buzzed. I looked down, saw Bay Breeze Inn pop up on the caller ID, and hit speaker. "Frank Hardy."

"Hey, Frank, it's Sophie over at Bay Breeze. Just wanted to let you know that Mr. Bishop just got back and went to his room," Sophie's bubbly voice chirped into the room over the speaker.

I looked up at Joe, who was already pulling his jacket on, ready to roll for the Bay Breeze.

"That's great, Sophie, thanks!"

"Sure thing," she said. "Mr. Bishop sure is a popular guy for such a sourpuss. Someone else came by from the museum looking for him too."

My antennae shot up.

"Was it Mr. Lakin? You know, the history teacher from Bayport High?" I blurted. If it was our fugitive teacher, Sophie could have just broken the whole case open for us.

"You mean the old guy with tacky thrift-store suits?" Sophie asked.

"Yeah, him!" I almost shouted in anticipation.

"Nah," she said, popping her gum and bursting our balloon.

"It was some other guy. Real big guy too. He had some kind of military tattoo on his arm."

SHANGHAIED 16

JOE

REAL BIG GUY WITH A MILITARY TATTOO on his arm? *Ding.* The phone call from the Bay Breeze just got a lot more interesting—the guy Sophie had described sounded like somebody else we knew.

"Was his name Bernie, Bernie Blank?" Frank asked Sophie.

"He didn't say, just said he was from the museum and told me to tell Mr. Bishop he'd be waiting at Barnacle Bill's. Said Mr. Bishop'd know what it was about," she replied. Barnacle Bill's was the local dive on the pier across from the arcade.

"You want me to ring up Mr. Bishop's room for you?" Sophie asked.

"Nah, I think we'd rather surprise him. Thanks, Sophie, we owe you one." Frank clicked off.

We might have just gotten a huge break in the case, but Frank looked apprehensive. Our last attempt to talk to Bernie hadn't exactly gone smoothly.

"Sophie was right about Bishop being a popular guy," I said. "It seems like everybody on the museum side of this case wanted to meet him."

Frank frowned. "Yeah, and it hasn't turned out too well for them either. One's dead and another's missing. I wonder what's in store for Bernie."

"Well, at least we know he can defend himself," I joked, but Frank didn't seem to appreciate my attempt at humor.

"If it is Bernie, what do you think he wants with Bishop?" I asked, trying to piece together how the intimidating ex-soldier fit into our puzzle.

"Whatever it is, I don't think it's a coincidence," Frank replied.

"Well, we've got two hot leads at two different locations. Only way to follow them both is to split up. I'll take Bernie, you go after Bishop," I offered. I knew my brother wasn't excited about the possibility of accidentally surprising Bernie after what happened the last time one of us snuck up on him.

"I don't like it, Joe," Frank said. "I think we should stick together."

"I don't like it either, but we're running out of time, and this is the only chance we have to stay on top of both leads," I reminded him.

Frank thought about it for a second before conceding.

"Fine, but don't get too close and don't stick your neck out with Bernie or anyone else. Just keep an eye on him and see what he does," he cautioned. I didn't like seeing him stressing over me, but it's good knowing your brother is looking out for you.

"That's the plan, bro. I like my neck even more than I like yours," I joked, hoping to lighten the mood. "Besides, if he's at Barnacle Bill's, the arcade is the perfect place to pull surveillance. There will be plenty of other people around, and even if he spots me, there's nothing suspicious about me wasting quarters in the arcade."

"Stay safe," he said, nodding reluctantly. "The Bay Breeze is just a few blocks from the pier. Any sign of trouble, holler and I'm there."

"You too and likewise," I told him.

Frank fixed me with a serious stare. "Now let's crack this thing wide open."

I smiled. That's what I wanted to hear. "Let's do it."

Frank headed left toward the Bay Breeze, and I headed right toward the pier where Barnacle Bill's was. Unfortunately, Bernie wasn't there. I posted myself by the pinball machines and wasted a few quarters like I'd told Frank I would, but there was no sign of Bernie. We were running out of time and I was running out of patience, so I ducked my head inside the Barnacle for a closer look and then went right ahead and asked a couple of the locals when it was clear Bernie wasn't there. They said Bernie had gotten a call and taken off before I got there. I sure would have liked to know who was on the other end of the line and what it was they said. Out of ideas, I headed for the Bay Breeze to meet up with Frank and see if he'd had better luck finding Bishop.

I could see the *Resolve* from the pier as I walked back. Frank was right, it was a pretty amazing sight. I stopped for a second to admire it, when something unusual caught my eye. It was hard to tell what they were doing from that distance, but it looked like there was someone on deck. That was strange. It was after hours, and with the museum shut down by Chief Olaf until the murder investigation was over, there shouldn't have been anyone onboard. I gave it some thought and kept walking, assuming it was probably just one of the officers. I didn't get far though before curiosity got the better of me. I figured it couldn't hurt to stay in the shadows and sneak a closer look before meeting up with Frank.

By the time I got close enough to make out what was happening on deck, whoever had been there was gone. I was about to write it off and head back when a creaking noise stopped me. At first I thought my eyes were playing tricks on me when one of the *Resolve*'s wooden dinghies started inching its way up the side of the ship. The notion of ghosts popped its way back into my mind, and I popped it out just as fast. I couldn't see anyone from my vantage point, but someone must have been using a winch to haul the dinghy back up to the deck. Now that really was strange. No police officer would be on the *Resolve* alone at night, loading and unloading dinghies.

I hid behind one of the dock's giant decorative anchors in case anyone was watching. I couldn't see what was going on, but I could hear someone securing the dinghy to its place on the deck. I crept along the dock to get a closer look at the waterline where the dinghy had come from. There was another small boat tied to the dock, hidden in the shadow of the ship, and this one wasn't two centuries old. It was a modern motorboat, loaded with what looked like duffel bags, and it was parked out of view in a place where it definitely shouldn't have been. It was positioned perfectly so it couldn't be seen from the public dock and wouldn't be spotted from a passing boat without a spotlight. Whoever had parked it there hadn't wanted it to be found. The boat appeared to be empty besides the bags. I gave a look around and then glanced back up toward the deck of the ship where the dinghy was. There was no one in sight, so I decided to do a little bit of quick reconnaissance.

I double-checked just to be sure no one could see me, then hopped aboard the motorboat. It bobbed up and down in the current, and I carefully made my way across the bow to get a closer look at its cargo: a neatly stacked pile of large black duffel bags. I gave one a tug by the handles, and it barely budged. The bags were heavy enough to be filled to the gills with muskets or maybe even one of the *Resolve*'s smaller cannons. Was somebody really gutsy enough to try to rob the museum right under the cops' noses during a full-blown criminal investigation? I wasn't about to let them get away with it if they were.

I leaned down, grabbed the zipper, and started to pull. The zipper barely made it an inch before something heavy slammed into me from behind, knocking the wind clean out of me. Stars exploded in my head, and I gasped for breath. It felt like an anchor had dropped on me. An anchor would have been preferable. The last thing I saw before everything went black was the Marine Corps tattoo on the huge forearm crushing my windpipe.

UNLOCKED 17

FRANK

I HAD JUST MADE IT TO THE BAY BREEZE INN when Dirk Bishop stepped out of his hotel room, carrying a large leather briefcase. I ducked behind the corner so he wouldn't see me and let him get a good head start before tailing him from a safe distance as he hurried down the street in the direction of the harbor. He paused to look at his gold watch and continued on his way with a satisfied smirk, looking like he was up to no good.

It was getting late, and with the town on edge over the Don's murder, there weren't many people out at night. It's easier to tail someone without getting made if there are a lot of other people around to distract your mark, so I had to be extra careful that Bishop didn't catch on. I followed him from far enough back that I could still see him, yet if he turned around and caught a glimpse of someone on the path behind him, he wouldn't recognize me or be suspicious. That was the idea, at least.

Bishop continued toward the harbor, and soon I could see the *Resolve*'s masts looming over the other vessels. When the grand old warship came into view, Bishop gave a furtive look around as if to make sure he wasn't being followed and then picked up his pace. Luckily, I had slipped off the path just in time so he didn't see me.

Yup, there was no doubt about it, Bishop was headed straight for the *Resolve*. Now that I knew the where and when of Bishop's little stroll, I was even more curious to learn the who, what, and why.

A more pressing question surfaced as soon as I got closer to the ship. Bishop had stopped at one of the benches farther down the dock, where he checked his watch and started looking around like he was waiting for someone. But at that moment I was less concerned about Bishop than what I saw on the deck of the *Resolve*. Bishop hadn't seen what I had. It was too dark to make out clearly, but the silhouettes of the big guy with the little guy slung over his shoulder like a sack of potatoes looked a whole lot like Bernie and my brother.

I forgot all about Bishop and sprinted for the ship. Bishop was busy looking in the other direction so he didn't see me, not that I really cared if he did. Getting to Joe, if that really was Joe I'd just seen slumped over the big man's shoulder, was a lot more important.

The gate from the dock to the gangplank was unlocked, which it shouldn't have been, and I slipped inside and up the plank onto the *Resolve*. When I got there, whoever had been on the deck was gone. All that was left were the eerie sounds of windblown chains and rope slapping against wood and the ominous shadows cast by cannons and masts.

The *Resolve* was huge, and I didn't know where to begin searching. Joe had gone looking for Bernie, and the big silhouette I saw carrying the body across the deck certainly could have belonged to the hulking weapons specialist. If it had been Bernie, then the only logical destination I could think of was the armory. I shuddered. I'd already had one unpleasant run-in with Bernie Blank in that room, and I wasn't thrilled about the prospect of another. Thinking about Joe in peril was enough to get me to swallow my fear and push on.

Even in sneakers, my footsteps echoed off the wood floor in the empty ship a lot louder than I would have liked. Moonlight crept through the portals, giving me enough light to see, but made the ship look downright spooky. Tiptoeing through the gun deck, I was half-sure Bernie was going to leap out from the shadows and grab me.

The armory door was open, and I couldn't hear anything inside. I crept cautiously up to the door and sneaked a peek inside. Empty. Just cases filled with guns and sabers and other weapons. If I was going to confront Bernie again, this time I planned to be armed. A display containing an assortment of weapons worn by officers was unlocked—which, like the main gate, it shouldn't have been. I pulled a short cutlass-looking saber from the case and felt the weight of it in my hand. I was contemplating borrowing something more intimidating as well when I heard a muffled crashing noise from the back of the ship. I sprinted toward the sound, clutching the cutlass in my hand, praying I wasn't too late.

*

A WATERY GRAVE

18

JOE

WHEN I CAME TO, I WAS SLUNG OVER Bernie's shoulder with my hands tied behind my back. I tried to scream, but all that came out was a muffled moan. That's when I realized the muscle-bound jerk had gagged me as well. Man, was I angry at myself for getting snuck up on like that. I had been so focused on finding out what was in those bags, I'd let myself get ambushed. I was starting to think Frank had probably been right about not splitting up.

Bernie gave me a hard jab to the ribs with his elbow.

"Quiet," he snapped, then added, "Not that anyone can hear you anyway."

Well, that was encouraging. It wasn't going to stop me

from trying, though. I'd just have to be more clever about it. Which was going to prove tough while gagged and bound. It's a good thing I like a challenge.

I tried to get my bearings. We were deep below deck of the *Resolve* and going deeper. I recognized the big yellow DANGER sign in the corridor ahead. Bernie was headed for the dark no-man's-land in the construction zone at the back of the ship, where Frank and I had hidden from the cops the day before. Just great. Bernie might as well be taking me to an underground cave. No one was going to be able to find me there, definitely not before the morning, when and if the police returned to the ship to continue their investigation. I figured I'd better come up with a plan quick or no one would ever see me again. Not alive, at least. With my hands tied behind my back, I didn't have a lot of options, but an idea came to me. It was a stretch—literally—and I only had a split second to try it.

As soon as Bernie stepped past the caution tape into the construction zone, I stretched my hands away from my back as far as I could and tried to use the rope Bernie had wound around my wrists to snag the edge of the CONSTRUCTION ZONE—HARD HAT REQUIRED sign. The rope caught! Bernie's forward momentum yanked the sign down and sent it clattering to the floor. Yes! The sound echoed through the empty ship. It wasn't much of an emergency alarm, but it would have to do. I just hoped someone was within earshot to hear it.

I paid for my plan with another hard elbow to the ribs.

I gasped for breath and nearly choked on the gag in my mouth.

"Enough," Bernie warned. "I don't want to hurt you more than I have to."

Again, very reassuring. I wasn't about to stop trying to escape, though. It just didn't look like I was going to have the chance. It was pitch black in the construction zone, and Bernie didn't bother with lights. He navigated the darkness with no problem and barely made a sound on the creaky floor as he went. It was like he really was a ninja commando. It wasn't until I felt us descending a ladder that I realized where we were: the gaping jagged hole leading down to the cargo hold deep inside the ship.

This was where Frank said Mr. Lakin had found the crates full of artifacts. Here, even Bernie's ninja stealth couldn't stop the rotted wood floor from creaking under his feet. I'd been worried about falling through the floor when Frank and I were in the construction zone. Now, beneath Bernie's and my combined weight, I was about sure we were going to crash right through the bottom straight into the bay.

Bernie descended another even more rickety ladder before lugging me off his shoulder and tying me to a chair. A few seconds later, flickering orange light put an end to the darkness. Bernie had lit an old oil lantern, filling the chamber with a fiery glow.

"I'll take the gag off, but if you yell, I'll knock your teeth out before putting it back on," he declared.

"Mmmrkkyy," I replied affirmatively. I like my teeth. I didn't suffer through years of braces just to have them knocked out.

Bernie removed the gag, and I sucked in a deep breath of salty, musty air. I looked around at the crumbling ship walls and rotting floorboards. From down here, it seemed like a miracle the ship even stayed afloat at all. We were on the lower level of a dusty, empty storeroom that looked close to collapse. This must have been the old cargo hold Frank had been so eager to explore. Not that there was much left to see, really, just some empty crates and a frayed, rusty rope-and-pulley system that must have once been used to hoist heavy cargo up past the ladder Bernie had carried me down to the storage loft above. The notion of pulling myself up one of the ropes to safety crossed my mind and went *poof* instantly. That escape route was no good, not with my hands tied behind my back and Bernie between me and the rope.

Bernie was one of the bad guys, that much was clear, but I was still trying to figure out where he fit in with Don Sterling's murder, Mr. Lakin's disappearance, and Dirk Bishop's visit. Well, I wasn't going to get a better time to try and find out. It's not like I had anything else to do.

"So I guess now you get to finish what you started yesterday in the armory," I said. It probably wasn't smart to antagonize him, but I was itching for answers, and Frank is supposed to be the smart one anyway. Bernie grunted in response and gave me a funny look, like he didn't know what I was talking about.

"Frank was right about you," I went on. "The only reason you let him go yesterday was you realized I was there to witness you attacking him, and getting rid of two bodies would've been a lot harder than just one. What I don't get is why."

"That was an accident. I didn't mean to hurt your brother yesterday when he surprised me, and I don't want to hurt you," Bernie said, sounding oddly sincere. "You may not believe this, but I really am sorry about all this. I like you boys. You have guts. You just have a bad habit of being in the wrong place at the right time. It's too bad. You would have made good soldiers."

I didn't like Bernie's use of the past tense.

"You could still let me go, you know. Things will go a lot easier for you when you get caught if you don't harm a kid," I tried to reason with him.

"Let you go?" Bernie laughed. "Harming you is what is going to make it easier for me not to get caught. You've given me the perfect way to complete my cover."

That's when he pulled out one of the antique flintlock pistols he and Mr. Lakin had been carrying at the reenactment and aimed it at my heart.

AT ROPE'S END

19

FRANK

'D FOLLOWED THE CRASHING NOISE TO THE back of the ship past the King's Pride exhibit, where the renovations were still being finished. The CONSTRUCTION ZONE sign stared up at me from the floor like a big, bright, yellow bread crumb. Joe hadn't only left me a sign, he'd left me an actual sign! With a pun like that, I really was convinced it was my brother I'd seen carried across the deck of the ship.

I turned on my mobile flashlight and ducked past the caution tape into the dark, hoping I'd get lucky and stumble on Joe and his abductor before they stumbled on me. I just wasn't sure what I was going to do when I found them. I stopped when I reached the hole in the floor leading down to the cargo hold where Mr. Lakin had made his discovery, not really sure which direction to go from there. I had just started to head down the corridor where we'd found Mr. Lakin's old office when I thought I heard murmuring behind me. I stopped and listened. I couldn't hear what they were saying, but someone was definitely down there.

Yesterday I had been itching to go down and explore the cargo hold. Now that I had my chance, it seemed a lot less welcoming. I gathered myself and started down the ladder. When I reached the bottom, I quickly flipped off my light. The voices were louder, and there was a faint flicker of light coming from somewhere below.

The cargo hold was actually two stories, and I was in the loft overhanging the main hold. I crept cautiously to the edge, peeked out from behind an empty wooden crate, and looked down. From my hiding place I could see Joe with his hands tied behind him. There was a loud clicking noise, and my brother's eyes went as wide as ship portals. A few feet away stood the last person I wanted to see. Bernie Blank. And he had one of the big old black powder pistols in his hand, with the hammer half-cocked and ready to load.

I didn't have much time. Bernie could have the pistol loaded and ready to fire in under a minute. I had to act fast to save Joe. I just didn't have a clue how I was going to do it. I looked down at the short saber in my hand. Little good it would do me from up here. That's when the ropes caught my eye. They were hooked to the crate I was hiding behind and ran all the way up to the ancient iron pulley attached to the ceiling beam over Bernie's head. A plan started to form. *Keep him talking a little longer, Joe,* I thought. *Please keep him talking.*

THE BIG ZERO

20

JOE

JUST KEEP HIM TALKING, I THOUGHT as I stared down the barrel of the antique gun. There was a .75 caliber ball of 250-year-old hot lead coming my way if I didn't. Bernie had pulled out a powder horn and started loading the pistol with methodical precision. I didn't have much time. I don't know what I was stalling for, but I wasn't ready to bite the big one. Even if it meant just a few minutes between now and the Big Zero, as Frank called it, I was going to take it.

"We were onto you, you know. My brother and the police aren't going to let you get away with this," I bluffed.

"Sorry to disappoint you, but by the time anyone finds you, I'll be long gone," Bernie said calmly. "They won't even suspect me, and if they do, there won't be any proof. Or I guess I should say, there will be plenty of proof. It just won't point to me."

Bernie continued to load the pistol. I noticed for the first time that he was wearing gloves, and things started to click into place.

"Because the fingerprints on the gun aren't yours," I said, realization dawning.

Bernie looked up from the pistol. "Affirmative, private."

I studied the pistol in Bernie's hands. It was identical to the one Mr. Lakin had used—in fact, I realized, the chances were good that it was the very gun that had been fired by Mr. Lakin at the reenactment and that still had his fingerprints on it. And that same gun was aimed at me now.

One gun, two murders. Bernie would have pulled the trigger only once, but if his plan succeeded, no one would know that he had ever even held the gun at all. There would only be one set of fingerprints on it. My Second Man theory had just gotten a lot clearer. I had been right about there being a second person involved in Don Sterling's murder. I just hadn't been right about the shooter. Mikey had nothing to do with it.

"The gun isn't yours either, is it?" I asked. Bernie just grunted and withdrew the ramrod. "But this isn't the first time you loaded it with a musket ball."

"Good work, private. Not that it will do you much good." Bernie blew off the excess powder from the muzzle of the gun.

He might be right, but if I was going to go, I at least wanted to go solving the crime.

"The police are right about Mr. Lakin shooting Don Sterling," I told him.

Bernie smirked. "Even Chief Olaf gets something right every once in a while."

"They just don't know that Mr. Lakin's not the one who loaded the gun." I added the crucial piece of information. "Mr. Lakin shot the Don, but you're the one who put the musket ball down the barrel. The question is, did he know about it beforehand? Was Mr. Lakin your accomplice, or did you frame him for the Don's murder like you plan to frame him for mine?"

"Accomplice?" Bernie laughed. "The old man was clueless. He was a convenient patsy. Lakin was a cop and I was a soldier. We shared war stories. I knew he could shoot, and I knew he'd planned that little stunt with the horse to show up Sterling. Everybody knew they hated each other. He would be the obvious suspect if anything happened to the Don. He made it easy for me."

I rewound the scene from the battlefield in my mind. The people playing British and American officers hadn't loaded their pistols during the actual battle reenactment like the infantry had. They'd loaded them before the shooting started, like the real officers would have before heading into battle with their troops. So Mr. Lakin would have started out with his pistol safely loaded with only a blank charge.

I thought about the video Aunt Trudy shot of the reenactment, how Mr. Lakin had stood side by side with Bernie while they handed out the muskets. The camera had panned away while they were still standing there, so we didn't get to see what happened next. Not that we would have anyway. Bernie had quick hands.

"So you picked his pocket and swapped the gun he was wearing with yours, the one you'd secretly already loaded with a real musket ball." I broke down what I now knew had happened next. "Mr. Lakin executed the Don for you without even knowing it."

Bernie smiled. "Bull's-eye."

I usually appreciate a good pun. Not this time. I thought about how guilty Mikey had felt for even aiming at the Don, and my anger at Bernie got even hotter. Thankfully Mikey hadn't been involved, but Bernie's cruel plot would have made every one of the militiamen who had fired a gun during the reenactment question whether they were a killer. Especially Mr. Lakin. Imagine not only being framed for murder, but being turned into an unwitting assassin!

Bernie's smile turned to a scowl as he raised the pistol. "Now let's see if I'm as good a shot as your history teacher."

With the barrel leveled at my heart, my brain scrambled to come up with a good stall tactic. I doubted begging would do much good. I hated my next idea almost as much, but I had to try. If I couldn't reason with him, maybe I could flatter him. I swallowed my ego and tried to massage his.

"I have to give it to you, it's a pretty brilliant plan," I said, choking back my disgust. "Heck, just using the reenactment to disguise the murder was genius, even without all the other stuff. With all those people already firing guns in Don Sterling's direction, you could take him out in plain sight without anyone being the least bit suspicious. You knew how hard it would be to match the bullet back to the shooter even if you pulled the trigger yourself, but you were smart enough to add another layer of deception and put more distance between you and the murder weapon by having somebody else pull the trigger for you. The shooter didn't even have to know his gun was loaded for it to work, just so long as you knew they were going to aim at Don Sterling during the battle. The police will be chasing their tails forever. And so what if they do get a clue? They'll be looking at Mr. Lakin instead of you. They never would have guessed the real bad guy wasn't even the shooter."

My tactic worked. Bernie nodded at me approvingly.

"You're a sharp kid. It's a shame it has to end this way. In a perfect world, nobody else would have gotten hurt. Not even Lakin. The case would have gone cold before anyone solved it. These old smoothbore pistols don't leave markings. And even if the police did match up the gun, the evidence would point away from me. There was no reason for anyone to suspect me. Lakin was so convenient, it was perfect. But then he got inconvenient; he tried to talk to someone he wasn't supposed to and got in the way."

My relief that our history teacher wasn't the murderer was stripped away by a new reality.

"What did you do to him?" I snapped.

"I got him out of the way," Bernie replied simply.

"Everyone will just continue to think he went on the run from the police," I said, my hope fading as I realized how well Bernie had stacked the odds against justice.

"Works for me," Bernie said.

My heart sank. I didn't want to think about what Bernie had done to Mr. Lakin, but if I didn't figure out something quick, the same thing was going to happen to me. Bernie started to explain what he had in mind.

"Getting Lakin out of the way wasn't anything I couldn't handle, but it left some loose ends that would have been difficult for me to explain when the police came calling. Lucky for me, you showed up to help me tie everything up in a neat package for Olaf. I didn't want anyone else to get hurt, but you snooped your way into top secret intelligence. I can't allow it to fall into enemy hands, and sometimes a little collateral damage is necessary to complete a mission."

I thought I knew what the next objective in Bernie's mission was, and it didn't end happily for Joe Hardy.

"So when they find my body, they'll also find the pistol with Mr. Lakin's fingerprints on it. It'll be the same one he fired at the reenactment, so even if they can't match up the bullet from the Don's body, the police will assume he used it to shoot both of us. Case closed."

"They'll even find the entry wound in the exact same place on both bodies," Bernie informed me.

My heart started beating faster. Apparently it wasn't ready to take a bullet. *Keep stalling, Joe Hardy!* yelled the voice in my head.

"But—" I started as my mind raced to come with up with something else to keep him talking.

"I'm sorry, kid. It's time we end this conversation. I have a rendezvous to get to," Bernie said, and raised the gun again.

"Bishop," I blurted.

Bernie lowered the gun a little and fixed me with a stare.

"That's who you wanted to stop Mr. Lakin from talking to. And Don Sterling. Bishop is who you're going to rendezvous with now too, isn't it?"

"You boys have been busy, haven't you? I think I underestimated you. I'm not going to make the same mistake again," Bernie said as he started to thumb back the hammer.

"Wait! You still haven't told me why you wanted Don Sterling dead. You didn't have any beef with him, not that anyone knew about."

"Because Don got greedy and didn't want to share. I found something he didn't want me to. He could have been generous, but he decided to go behind my back and try to cut me out."

"So you cut him out instead. The same with Mr. Lakin when he tried to talk to Bishop. That way you could keep Bishop to yourself without anyone else getting in the way."

I got a sinking feeling when I realized that Frank and I were the ones who'd told Bishop to talk to Mr. Lakin. The crime was coming full circle, and it all ran through the Englishman. I sure hoped Frank was having better luck with him than I was with Bernie. Bernie had already gotten rid of everyone else who had tried to meet with Bishop, and the only upside of me being on the other end of Bernie's pistol was it meant he was here with me, and my brother was safe for the time being.

Just then an alarm went off on the military watch wrapped around Bernie's thick wrist. He glanced down.

"It's time to go," he said. "The rest will just have to stay a mystery."

I didn't even have time to reply. In one fluid motion Bernie took aim, cocked the hammer all the way back, and pulled the trigger.

I stood there, hands tied, looking down the barrel, watching helplessly as the flint-tipped hammer hit metal, igniting the powder in the pan. People say you see your life flash in front of your eyes. Not for me. Time did seem to freeze, though, that much is true, and everything on the ship seemed to go all quiet, like it was just me and the muzzle and my final thoughts. I thought about missing Aunt Trudy's cooking and my dad's after-dinner lessons on proper investigative protocol. I thought about how lucky I was to have had teachers like Mr. Lakin, and I thought about Jen and how much it stunk that I wouldn't get to see if things would work out for us. And Mikey, too, about not getting a chance to tell him he didn't kill the Don after all, so he wouldn't feel so bad. Mostly I thought about how proud I was to have been one of the Hardy boys and how much I was going to miss solving mysteries with my brother Frank.

The last thing I saw were the flames leaping toward me from the muzzle of the gun. I barely even heard the shot.

SWASHBUCKLED 21

FRANK

THE FEW MINUTES BEFORE THE GUN-
shot went off seemed like the longest of my
life. I knew that if I didn't do something
quickly, they were going to be Joe's last. My
brother was doing a great job of stalling, but I
was running out of time.

As I scrambled to come up with a plan before Bernie
pulled the trigger, the rope and the cutlass had sparked
a totally unexpected memory—the dream I'd had earlier
about rescuing Daphne from the pirate who looked like
Mr. Lakin!

Okay, so before you start thinking I'd lost my mind, day-
dreaming pirate fantasies while my brother was about to be
gunned down by a cold-blooded killer, let me explain. In

the dream, I'd been swinging from a rope across the bow of the ship with a cutlass clenched between my teeth. Get it? Even with Joe being held at gunpoint below, I had to smile to myself. Who says dreams don't come true?

Okay, so Joe didn't make nearly as pretty a damsel in distress, and Bernie made a much more frightening villain, but it still just might work. We were also deep inside the hull instead of on deck, but I still had the main ingredients for a daring rescue—the rope attached to the ceiling and the cutlass I'd taken from the armory.

On closer inspection, the crate I was hiding behind was actually a big bin used to lift cargo between the two levels. There were a couple of large duffel bags inside, but I wasn't concerned with the bin's contents. I was focused on the ropes running from the bin up to the ceiling beam over Bernie's head. I gave one of the ropes a tug, and it held tight. Good. That meant the rope was securely attached to the beam and would support my weight so I could swing from it. That's what I hoped, at least.

I did some rapid calculations in my head. Distance. Angle. Velocity. If I was right, the rope would hold and I'd have just enough of it to reach Bernie, taking him out before he could shoot Joe.

I looked down across the cargo hold at my target. The height made my head spin, and my heart was thump-thump-thumping so loud I was afraid Bernie would hear. If I was wrong, I'd miss Bernie, or worse, end up careening to the floor with nothing to break my fall, and then both Hardy boys would be kaput.

The alarm on Bernie's watch went off.

"It's time to go," I heard Bernie say to Joe.

No time to second-guess. I made sure I had a good grip on the rope with one hand, raised the cutlass to cut the rope free with the other, and . . .

"The rest will just have to stay . . . ," Bernie began.

"Now, Frank!" my brain screamed . . .

". . . a mystery."

Just as Bernie raised the gun to shoot Joe, I thwacked the cutlass through the rope, chomped down on the blade, and *SWUNG*.

For one awesome split second it felt like I was flying as I swung through the air across the cargo hold. A split second later the rope went slack in my hands, and I was hurtling toward the ground like I'd been shot from a cannon. The ceiling beam I was swinging from had snapped!

A split second after that two things happened at once: The gun went off and I slammed into Bernie with the force of a human cannonball. The pistol jerked free of his hand and went flying, flames still pouring from the muzzle. Bernie and I went flying as well, tumbling across the floor in a tangle of arms and legs. I thought I heard a scream—oh no, Joe!—but I didn't have time to finish processing the thought. The broken beam was hurtling toward us like a missile, and it was pulling the cargo bin and duffel bags soaring through the air along behind it in an all-out aerial assault.

I was pinned under Bernie, unable to move, a sitting duck primed for the plucking. But this time Bernie's size worked to my advantage—I had my own hulking human shield. He threw up his arms like he meant to block the beam. His arms were big. The beam was bigger. The beam won. It smashed into him, and I went free-falling through the air for the second time in under a minute as the rotted wood caved in beneath us and we both smashed straight through the floor. We landed in a heap not far below, and everything started to go dark as we were swallowed in a cloud of centuries-old dust. My ears were ringing so loudly from the gunshot, I could barely even hear all the debris crashing down around me.

It was strange, though. For a second I imagined there were hundreds and hundreds of gold coins falling from the sky, and then Joe looking down on me like an angel from above, calling out softly as if in a dream, "Frank, Frank."

HISTORY, REVISED

22

JOE

T MAY HAVE BEEN MY IMAGINATION, BUT I SWEAR I was able to see the musket ball flying at me in slow motion. I shut my eyes, hoping to block it out like a bad dream. The darkness was filled with the explosion of the gunshot, the smell of gunpowder, and a cacophonous crashing noise. With all the chaos echoing around me, it sounded like I was back in the middle of the reenactment all over again. Was I having some sort of weird flashback on the way to the great beyond? I opened my eyes expecting to see clouds or cherubs with wings or whatever it is you see when you get to heaven, but if this was heaven, it was really dusty.

I blinked the dust out of my eyes. It looked like I was still onboard the *Resolve*. The awful thought crossed my mind that I had turned into one of the *Resolve*'s fabled ghosts, doomed to forever haunt the ship and scare kids like me. I frantically patted myself down, looking for bullet holes, but couldn't find any. I was still alive! And in one piece! But where was Bernie? The place where he'd been trying to shoot me from a few seconds earlier had been replaced by a giant hole in the floor. I looked around and noticed a much smaller hole just an inch or two to the left of my head, the size of .75 caliber musket ball. The wood was singed, and smoke still trickled out from the bullet hole. Talk about a close call!

I cautiously made my way across the room to the hole where Bernie had been and peered down. Was that Frank? And was he lying in a pile of gold coins? I had to be having some kind of bizarre near-death experience, right? Nope. The dust started to settle and there was Frank, looking dazed, his fall broken by Bernie, who was knocked out with a giant goose egg growing out of his oversize skull. A couple of the black duffel bags like the ones I'd seen on the motorboat had torn open around them, filling the hidden chamber beneath the collapsed cargo-hold floor with what could only be the King's Pride Treasure. Way to go, bro!

That wasn't all, though. Frank had done more than just rescue me, knock out the villain, and find the stolen gold. There was someone else down there with them. It was hard to tell with all the dust, but it looked like there was an old guy in a powder-blue plaid suit bound and gagged in the corner of the room. Was that . . . Mr. Lakin! And he was alive! When

Bernie had told me that he'd gotten Mr. Lakin "out of the way," I'd assumed the worst. But our history teacher wasn't dead. He'd been tied up down here the whole time.

"Frank!" I called down. "Brother, it sure is good to see you. Are you okay?"

"Joe?" he asked as he struggled to sit up. "Is that really you? I thought you were an angel."

I laughed. "That's funny. A second ago, I was sure I was a ghost."

A minute later I had climbed down into the hidden chamber and was helping my brother up. He was a bit dazed and bruised, but otherwise A-OK. As we tied up Bernie and untied Mr. Lakin, we were able to piece together what had happened.

Mr. Lakin had been drugged by Bernie and was pretty much still incommunicado. The last thing he seemed to remember was being hit from behind while on his way to see Dirk Bishop. He didn't know it had been Bernie who had kidnapped him or that he had been framed for murder, and he didn't seem to have a clue about the treasure, either. What a relief that our favorite history teacher was innocent.

He was pretty shocked to wake up in a hidden chamber under the cargo hold of the *Resolve*, surrounded by gold coins. The King's Pride Treasure was real, and it had been hidden right here aboard the *Resolve* for more than two centuries before Don Sterling found it and Bernie stole it from him. Who would have thought that all these years after

Frank and I used to play treasure hunters and pirates looking for the legendary lost gold as kids that we'd be the ones to actually recover it? Pretty cool, huh? We had written a new chapter for the history books after all. Maybe we'd even get our own display in the museum.

I put my arm around Frank. "It sure is good to be alive."

And man, did I mean it. There's nothing like a close call with a musket ball to make you really appreciate things. I was going to make sure to give Dad and Aunt Trudy big bear hugs when we got home. I was looking forward to telling Mikey he wasn't the shooter, too. Maybe he'd put in a good word for me with his sister. I was really kind of hoping Jen and I could start over now that I'd helped clear her brother's name.

By the time we it made back up onto the deck of the *Resolve*, Bishop and his briefcase were long gone. You could see the bullet hole in the side of the ship where the ball had missed me and passed all the way through the hull. We figured Bishop had been getting ready to buy the treasure from Bernie, but had probably heard the shot and taken off running for the first flight back to jolly old England. I had a feeling we hadn't seen the last of him, but for tonight our work was done.

When Chief Olaf finally arrived (late, as usual), the first thing he saw was Bernie Blank tied up on the dock, guarded by a groggy Mr. Lakin.

"Rollie?" he asked in disbelief.

"Evening, Chief," Mr. Lakin said, and hiccuped.

Then the chief looked up on the deck of the *Resolve* and saw Frank and me.

"Hardys! I demand to know what is going on here!" For some reason Chief Olaf never seems happy to see us.

"Sorry, Chief," I called back down. "We know you said you'd arrest us if we went near the ship, but we figured you might be willing to give us another get-out-of-jail-free card in exchange for the real killer."

"And Bayport's legendary long-lost treasure," Frank added, flipping one of the gold coins high in the air and catching it in his palm.

The chief just sighed and shook his head.

A photographer from the *Bayport Bugle* had shown up as well, and the next morning the paper ran a picture of the Hardy boys on the front page. Our clothes were torn and tattered, but we had big grins on our faces as we stood triumphantly by one of the cannons, looking like patriotic pirates with our cutlasses, old George Washington hats, and a heaping pile of gold treasure.